No

Lollie

ISBN: 1499731302

ISBN-13: 9781499731309

Plan for Grace

The decision was made. Grace Winston had no choice but to have the bone marrow transplant she needed for the aplastic anemia that afflicted her. The circumstances around the cancer and the cure were purely evil. Graham Sinclair, her boss of sorts, felt indebted to Grace for having saved his son's life in Ireland. Little did he know that he had made a deal with the devil for the bone marrow to save her life.

While everyone prepared for the procedure, Sinclair pulled Travis to the side. He felt obligated to tell the new husband about the donor of her bone marrow. As her husband, he could make a decision about Shawn Sorenson.

"He is an evil man, Travis," Graham reiterated after explaining how he found Grace's brother vindictive and wicked. "Talking with him made the hairs on my neck stand on end."

"Grace never talked about him. I wouldn't have known about him had I not heard her uncle mention him. I vaguely remembered that. She never has been forthcoming about her family. Well, I am glad he was willing to save her life. What brother wouldn't do that for their sister? I know I would give mine anything I have to save her life."

"This one would not. He was not exactly willing to do this procedure without a little incentive."

Travis questioned with a frown. "What do you mean incentive?"

"He was content to let her die, unless he was paid for his services."

"You are kidding!" Travis burst forth.

"I am afraid that I am not. He is demanding fifty thousand dollars in return for his bone marrow."

"Oh my. How am I ever going to tell Grace that I can't, that she can't have this done?" In his disbelief, he silently prayed for help from the Master.

"That is not your concern. What I need from you is permission to give the man his demands in order to save your wife's life," Mr. Sinclair urged quietly.

"But I could never repay you that kind of money. That is really too much to ask," protested the husband. "I appreciate it more than you will ever know; but really, I must not indebt myself to you in that capacity." Travis thrust his hands angrily into his pockets. How dare this brother be so cruel! He *could* indebt himself for Grace's life.

Mr. Sinclair became urgent, "Young man, I understand your pride, but you haven't a choice. This isn't your debt. I owe Miss Sorenson; I mean Grace, more than a measly fifty thousand dollars. If anything, I owe her much more. My son's life, is it not worth your wife's?"

"I don't understand."

"Indeed, you do not, but Grace does. She would never agree to let me return favor for her actions, so I plead with you to allow me this minor payment for what she did for David. Time is of the essence. We must not stand around arguing too long. The surgery is already scheduled."

Travis complied. He would work to his grave to pay the man back. All that mattered was getting this transplant for his wife.

"One more thing," Graham Sinclair added solemnly. "She is to never know about this transaction. You must give me your word that you'll never mention this to anyone."

"You have my word," he affirmed.

Prior arrangement was made that neither donor or recipient

would be placed in the same room. If it were necessary, then they would be put together, only after both were under anesthesia. Sinclair, guarding his every move, brought Shawn to the hospital. He would take no chances with this snake in the grass.

When the procedure was completed and the move was safe, Graham Sinclair flew Shawn to his hometown hospital in his own private plane to recuperate. That is where he paid the man the remainder of money required with a warning to never show his face around Grace, or he would suffer the consequences.

With this surgery having been completed, Grace readied to face the next battle. They planned the next surgery for Tuesday of the following week. Her body was weak, but could only get stronger with the tumor taken out.

Ruth and Isaiah offered to take Grace's foster daughter, Amy, back to Springfield on Sunday, so she would miss no more school. This they did and returned on that Tuesday for the surgery. The older Scottish couple were getting on in age and the worry of their special girl was wearing on them.

Isaiah watched out the window, silently, while Ruth knitted. Albert Jameston and Graham Sinclair spoke in solemn low tones, while their wives quietly chatted among themselves.

Jameston, like Sinclair, was a businessman that financed the foundation where Grace worked. Both men respected the woman and the work she had done for the children. They knew her work was far from over. There were many children out there in need of this particular advocate.

Travis paced the floor, stopped to stare out the other window, and then paced some more with a continual prayer in his heart.

During one of his window stops, Graham approached the worried husband. "She'll be alright, now. Don't worry. This is the best hospital in the United States. They do this procedure every day."

"I know, but, I just found my wife. We have spent entirely too much time apart. I cannot stand the thought of losing her now."

Graham smiled, "I can understand that. Tell me, now that you two finally hitched up, where do you intend to live? I mean, she lives on the West Coast, and you live on the East Coast. Will you move, or will she?"

"Grace is rooted in her work in Oregon. I could never ask her to give all that up. I, on the other hand, gave up my job to be here with her. Therefore, the logical move is mine."

6

"I see. I am sure she'll appreciate that."

Travis nodded, "We have not even gotten far enough to discuss it, yet. There are a great many things we must discuss, but there will be plenty of time for that."

"I can relieve you of one worry, that is, if you agree. I have a corporate office in Eugene, Oregon. Yesterday, my vice-president of operations in that branch, Bradley, was killed in an accident. I would really appreciate someone in that position whom I could trust. The president, Ron Singleton, is a tough cookie, but if you do your job, he is no problem. What do you say? Would you be interested? It pays well, with excellent benefits. You would not have to worry about Grace's medical bills."

"Quite frankly sir, I am not sure if I would know what to do. I have never held an office position before. My work has always been menial labor."

"Super! I need a hard working man. I am afraid my former vice president was getting slack in his duties. It would prove me well to have a man of your character in that position."

Travis held his hand out. "You have yourself a deal, Mr. Sinclair, if you do not mind my inexperience. Wait till I tell Grace!"

7

Michelle in Need of Grace

The surgery was long and tedious, but at last it was complete. The doctor came out in his scrubs to give details to the family members. They were not able to extract the whole tumor because of the way it was entwined with her nerves. He was hoping radiation would kill the remainder. The pressure of the tumor was responsible for the headaches, but she would not be free from them until all the legs of the tumor, which pinched the nerves, were destroyed. He informed them that most of her suffering was in the past.

One could hear the rejoicing down the hall. Praises were shouted to the Healer of all things. It was He who had touched their beloved. They waited in angst for the nurses to tell them she was out of recovery. Jameston and Sinclair, and their wives, took their leave of the jubilation in order to return to work. Their little lady was safe now.

Two days had passed, and Grace was gaining her strength. Color crept back to her cheeks, however dull it may have been. This battle was won, but the war was far from over. The next step was to take a certain amount of radiation treatments. While one spouse looked to this as a wonderful thing, the other spouse dreaded the process. Grace knew the repercussions of these treatments. She was antsy to go home. She could rest and recuperate so much better on the farm with her loved ones at her side. Now, she had a daughter to guide and help, which she was looking forward to.

Ruth and Isaiah headed home when the surgery was over, and they had found their Lamby to be safe once again. Isaiah mentioned his need to get back to his fields. He had been away entirely too long. The doctor had come in and told Grace that the bone marrow had taken, and for now, the aplastic anemia was in remission. Again, they shouted their praise unto God.

Grace's doting husband never left her side, except to shower and change. For this, he never left the hospital. He had finally achieved ultimate exultation in marrying Grace. He was made whole when Christ came into his heart, and his life was complete when Grace became his wife.

Several days after the surgery Renee called to report a bit of important news to Travis. She could not bear to tell Grace of the sad news. As he listened, the husband contemplated whether he should tell his new bride in her condition, but it was a short-lived debate, because Grace could read in his face that something was amiss. He could not hide it from her.

Per her demand, he sadly explained, "That was Renee. She was not sure whether she should tell you, but Ruth insisted. I fear to tell you in the shape you are in."

"Travis, what is it? I am no weakling that I cannot take a little bad news."

He rubbed her hand to comfort her as he told her. "It is about Michelle."

"Tell me they did not go behind my back and put her back with her dad," she panicked. Michelle was her latest rescue. She had stayed with Grace briefly, and Grace knew what the little girl had been through with her dad.

"It gets worse than that, I am afraid. They did send her home. Grace, five nights ago, she shot and killed her father. They are holding her in jail," he continued.

"In jail!"

"They are going to try her as an adult."

Grace threw back the covers from her body. "Travis, she is only eleven years old. Is anyone trying to get her out of there? Oh my goodness. That poor child." While she spoke, she was rummaging through the tiny closet for her clothes.

"And exactly what do you think you are doing?" he asked.

"I am going home. That child needs someone, and there is no one else to whom she can turn."

"See, that is why I didn't want to tell you. I knew you would not listen to reason. You cannot leave the hospital right now."

"You are my husband, and I am in submission to you, but this is one thing I must do. She is a baby. She is all alone and scared. Surely you must understand that. I am past the worst part now. I can do the treatments in Oregon just as easily as I can here. Please don't fight me on this."

Travis threw his hands up in surrender. "I knew before I married you that you were independent and strong willed. I can't fault you for what I admire about you. We'll go together. It is only been a few days, since you had major surgery. Are you sure you are strong enough?"

"Plenty. We need to make plane reservations. I do not know how much cash I have available, but I'll call Ruth to wire me what I have saved."

"No need, my love. I haven't had a chance to tell you the wonderful news. Mr. Sinclair gave me a job at his Eugene office. For starters, I have unlimited flying privileges. I don't think we will have a problem getting home." He put his hands on her shoulders to stop her. "I will agree to your decision under the condition that you listen to the doctor and take it easy. I'll not visit you in the hospital anymore. If you don't give me your word, I'll not put my approval on this early release."

"Praise the Lord, for His mercy endureth forever. Let's go home."

Travis liked the sound of that. Home. His home with Grace, but his mind was preparing as he rejoiced. He wanted Wendy to be there also. It was time Wendy met her. She would fall in love with Grace as he had done. She could be a good influence to Amy. He hoped she would enjoy having a new sister. He had the idea to invite his cousin, Brad and his family to bring Wendy to his new home. Terry was a nurse and could keep an eye on his beloved.

Sinclair met them in his private plane so Grace could get the proper rest and he could acquaint Travis with his new position. Jameston forbade her to return to work for at least another two months. He determined she would get better before attempting work. He knew she would take care of Michelle, but other than that, she was to boycott work.

On the flight home, Travis enlightened his new wife on his ideas. "Would it be too much on you if I invited my cousin and his wife to stay with us for a few days? Do you remember Brad? I was hoping they would bring my daughter so that she could meet you. Albeit, if you are not up to it, I understand."

Grace smiled a hint of her former charm, "It is your home as well as mine. You may invite whom you will. I have been waiting to meet your daughter."

"I don't know what I could possibly have done to deserve you, but I thank God for you," he told her as he caressed her hand. A few minutes of thought brought a furrow across his brow. "Grace, what are you going to do about Michelle? I mean, you are in no condition to do a lot."

"I intend to pray first. Then, I intend to get that child safely home. She cannot stay in there, Travis. She is only a child."

With her hand still in his, Travis bowed and prayed with his new wife for wisdom from above. There was nothing God could not do. Sinclair watched them curiously. Was this different belief that Grace had the reason she was extraordinary? Even in adversity, the girl was at peace. David told him of their conversation about one having to be born again to enter heaven. That was very contrary to the catholic faith. Yet, this incredible person, who was dying, was literally happy to go. He settled in his heart to investigate this matter further. Maybe he and his wife needed to make some changes in the way of their worship.

Grace for Every Trial

The dead of winter had peaked in Oregon. The snow covered field glistened as in the Christmas carol, *Winter Wonderland*. Samson cleared the fence at the sight of his mistress. It had been entirely too long since she had fed him a carrot or apple. Where had she been? He thought she had abandoned him; she had been gone so long. He reached her before she reached the porch and snorted his welcome.

"Hey big boy. What have you been up to?" She patted him gently, stroking his shiny coat. "It looks like Renee has been feeding you good. Look at you. How would you like to go for a ride later on?"

He nuzzled her in approval as if to say, "Now would be fine." However, Isaiah took him back to the barn, much to his dismay.

Renee hugged Grace until Amy wedged her way between them. "Momma, what are you doing here so soon? We did not expect you at all."

"I have been away too long, young lady. It is about time I attend to my new daughter. Wild horses could not have kept me away any longer."

"Mr. Sinclair, welcoom to our home." Ruth greeted.

"Thank you, Ruth. It sure is beautiful in Oregon. I don' t make it out this way very often. I sure appreciate your hospitality."

Ruth beamed. She had the foresight of knowing Lamby. The minute Grace found out about Michelle, she knew her Lamby would come running. She had prepared a feast fit for a king. The fact that one more mouth to feed was there did not faze her in the least. There was plenty.

Brad was unable to take off until the next weekend. He and Terry had just taken a week's vacation shortly before Christmas, much to his regret, but they did get excited about visiting a new part of the country, even if it was for a couple days. Travis sent four plane tickets for them, Wendy, and their daughter, Stacy. He left out the fact that he and Grace had gotten married. He was not sure how Wendy would take such news over the phone.

The first thing Grace did was to slip into her study and call Stephanie to find Michelle. "Stephanie, why is Michelle in jail? Why did someone not stop her from being put in jail, for Pete's sake? She is only a babe."

"Grace, how wonderful to hear from you. How are you feeling?"

16

"Very angry. How could you let this happen?"

"Grace, slow down, now. I tried everything I could, but they wouldn't listen. By her own admission, she killed him. According to her confession, she had malice and forethought. They are going for man one."

"Poppycock Stephanie. She is eleven years old. Did they not stop to think that if a child had the forethought to kill someone, there would be a good reason?"

"I suppose not."

"Where is she?"

Stephanie returned, "Springfield jail."

"Can I not get her released? How much bail is set?"

"It is a hefty one. Five hundred thousand."

Grace drew her brows together. "Why so much? Didn't you explain to the judge that she is no risk? I mean, where should she flee? Surely, they would not consider her a threat to anyone else."

"That is what I asked Judge Harris, before he silenced me short."

17

"Harris?" Grace responded, "How did he end up judge for this, I wonder? He has been mixed up in this from the beginning. I believe that fact is curious. Can you meet me at the courthouse in thirty minutes? I will see if I can come up with the cash."

"I'll be there. See you then."

"Thank you Stephanie. Bye."

Grace pressed her finger on the receiver button to disconnect the call. Letting it go, she pressed another set of numbers.

"Mr. Jameston. I have a problem. I know it is asking a lot of you, especially after everything you have done for me in the last little while. I would not ask it, if I knew of any other way."

"Name it."

"You take my entire pay, until it is paid back in full. I promise to repay every dime."

"How much do you need, Grace?" Jameston did not need to know any details. He knew if Grace was asking for it, then it was a necessity.

"I need to get Michelle out of jail. Her bail is set at five hundred thousand. I need ten percent of that. I have seven

18

hundred in savings, but I cannot come up with forty-nine thousand, three hundred on my own. I know it is asking a lot…"

Jameston interrupted, "It sounds to me like it is part of the business we are in. It is an expense for the foundation. You need not worry about paying it back, Grace. I will wire you the money. Give me time to get to the bank, and you shall have it. Where will you be to pick it up?"

Grace gave him all the important details and reiterated her intent on paying it all back. Then, she met Stephanie at the courthouse. Together, they went to the magistrate's office to post bail. Mr. Jameston had beaten them there. The money was already waiting for them.

The tear stained face of the eleven-year-old could not smile at Grace upon sight. Too long had she spent in this horrid place. Her sadness turned to exultation, when Grace told her she was taking her home with her, as she clung to the woman as if her very life were threatened.

That night, Grace held the girl firmly, reassuring her of her safety. Michelle fell asleep in her arms. This was the first time the girl had felt safe since the last time she was here. Even in her sleep, Michelle slipped out a few remaining sobs from her days of weeping. Travis and Grace slept in front of the fire that first night with Amy and Michelle snuggled on their laps. This is how they felt safe; this is how they stayed.

Grace did not return to the office just yet. The question of Michelle going to school needed to be resolved. The news had hit the papers, which meant everyone knew about the accusations. School would be very difficult for the girl. Home school was an option, if Grace gave up her work all together to stay home with her. Whatever decision was to be made, it could not be made overnight. Michelle was home, and that was all that was important.

The radiation treatments began on Thursday. The fair-haired Irish lass found them to be worse than the migraines. In fact, they would cause her severe headaches, along with the vomiting. Eating anything left a metal taste in her mouth, therefore, she had no desire to eat. She noticed how her appearance had already changed so drastically. She appeared old. Her hair was turning white and looked horrible, where they had shaved part of it for the surgery. Her face was green and old. She did not realize how age had crept up on her, until now. Her hands were thin and sallow, and the reflection of her body in the mirror looked ancient. Where did Grace go? "Who is this that stares back at me so frail," she asked.

Nonetheless, her husband's guests were coming on the morrow, and she must present a full healthy person before them. Meeting his daughter was especially frightening for Grace. She feared the girl would not appreciate the way her dad sneaked off to marry another woman, without even inviting her.

Grace trekked to her safe haven for the first time in a long while. Her prayer garden had begun to grow grass in the footpaths that were previously worn out. It was time to remake them. The comfort of this place brought a peace to her. Here, she could be still, and know God, as He commanded. She would listen for His direction, and she was at loss when it concerned Michelle. She had not asked any questions of the girl. She knew that when Michelle was ready, she would come on her own.

Another prayer that went up was for strength in suffering through the treatments. Grace was strong in the Lord, but the flesh was weak. She wanted to present her body wholly to her new family, instead of dependent upon them for support. She knew to lean on the One whom the winds and seas obey.

She thanked the Lord properly for giving her this new daughter. She knew not why it was to be that it would be short lived, but she did know God was in control of it all. "Help me," she prayed, "to be the mother and wife I should be. Help me to serve You in all that I do."

Lastly, she prayed for her dearly beloved Isaiah. All was not well with him. She prayed for wisdom and health for her sweet father figure. If God could spare him, she would gladly go in his stead.

After Sinclair introduced Travis to his new job the first two days, he flew home that Thursday morning, pleased with the choice he had made in the young man. It was time to let the newlyweds settle down into a daily routine as a family.

The trial for Michelle had not been set by Friday, so they decided that Michelle would stay at home to school until all the dust had settled. Ruth and Renee promised to oversee her education along with Grace. Ruth would help her when Grace and Renee were at work. Grace found the need to return to work to repay Mr. Jameston for his help. Without the knowledge of husband or boss, Grace planned that all of this would begin the following Monday. She would recover faster if she were busy doing something important.

Bountiful Grace

Grace had the forethought that Wendy would want some quality time alone with her father, without the rest of the family around. It would be a bitter pill to swallow to throw Amy and Grace on her at one time, so she made Travis meet his family alone at the airport on his way home from work.

Meanwhile, Grace found refuge from her anxiety on Samson's strong back. He had missed this rider tremendously, so without a saddle or bridle, she mounted, and the two trotted across the field, breaking into a gallop on occasion. Amy and Michelle were excitedly helping Ruth cook supper, and Isaiah was in the barn, watching the field for a sporadic glimpse of the black steed and its rider pass by.

Travis drove the visitors home in Grace's Mustang, which Brad scrutinized every detail. He, like most men, loved old cars, especially sports cars. He stood under the hood with Terry, while Travis took Wendy into Renee's house with the luggage. That was where Renee decided the couple would stay.

Then, he excitedly took Wendy by the hand to find Grace. Instead, he found the golden child with Michelle, helping Ruth. The introductions were made without letting Wendy know his relationship with Amy. He still wanted her to meet Grace first.

The snorting of what sounded to be a ferocious beast drew Brad and Terry's attention from under the hood of the sports car. The man pushed his wife protectively behind him, until he looked. Like a flash, a streak of black crossed the field behind the barn. The barely visible strawberry blond curls tipped the old cousin off to whom the rider was. He pulled his wife to the edge of the fence.

Brad let out a shrill whistle, which stopped Samson in his tracks. Was that some intruder? He turned his massive head toward the sound, and then took his mistress to the one who had made such a hideous sound. He stood snorting his disapproval of the intruders and shaking his head.

"Brad!" Grace exclaimed. "You are here. This must be your lovely wife."

"Yes," he introduced. "Terry, this is Grace. Grace, this is Terry. Who is the monster you are riding?" He pulled his hand back at Samson's angry snort.

Grace slid from the sleek black back. "This is Samson. You will have to overlook him. He gets a little territorial sometimes. I am afraid he tends to get a smidge jealous. Samson, stop that. You should be ashamed of yourself," she rebuked the black beauty.

24

Terry slipped her hand to pet the muzzle of the thoroughbred. He took to her gentle touch. Now, this, he could get used to. He did not like men who were nervous around him. This woman was like his mistress. She had a kind touch, void of fear and nervousness. She might bring him treats like Grace.

Before long, Terry had slipped between the split rails to pet the beast more thoroughly. Grace slipped her two sugar cubes to feed to him. "Yes," Samson thought, "I knew she'd bring me goodies."

"There you are." Travis strolled up with a perfectly shaped young woman. Her hair was darker than Travis's, but her eyes could not lie. They were the eyes of her father; bright twinkling brown eyes. She reminded Grace of a beautiful model or actress. She stood over Grace by a good shoulder length. It would have been intimidating to some other woman of Grace's height, but Grace was rarely intimidated.

"You must be Wendy," Grace extended her hand. She was ready to expand a handshake to a hug if permitted, but the girl would not even return her hand. "I have heard so much about you."

"Well, I have heard very little of you, from my dad anyway," she added with a bite.

Grace spoke quickly before Travis could reprimand the girl. It would not do to embarrass the girl at first impressions. "I am so glad you could come. Amy and Michelle have been looking forward to your coming as your father and I have been. Then there is Ruth. She is always tickled to have company. If you will come over to the barn, you will meet Isaiah. He doesn't say much, but he is a man of great wisdom. He has yet to meet someone he did not like."

Grace led Terry on her side of the fence, while Travis led Brad and Wendy on the other toward the barn. The ever-faithful Samson was not far behind. He wanted more of the petting he had received. Grace stole a glance at the seemingly perfect young face of the daughter. One flaw became evident. The pretty red lips had soured into a distasteful expression. It was evident she was not happy.

However, the scene in the barn turned nasty. The time had come for the truth to be told. It would only hurt to wait any longer. Travis came and stood beside his wife, putting his strong arm around her shoulders.

"Wendy, you are not meeting just an old friend of mine. Grace is my wife."

Wendy said nothing at first. The fire, which shot through

her glare, spoke louder than words. Brad reached his arm around Grace and his other hand out to his cousin.

"Well, congratulations man. When did this happen? Why did you keep it a secret? Didn't want your cousin to come in and steal her from you, did you?"

Travis laughed, "It was a quiet ceremony in New York. We did not feel right announcing it over the phone. We wanted to wait and tell you in person."

"Well, if you expect me to accept her as a mother, you are out of your mind, Dad. She will never be my mother." Wendy finally spoke before storming out of the barn.

The new husband looked questioningly at his wife, "Of course you should run after her. That is your job," was the look Grace returned. She had expected no less.

"You will have to overlook her Grace. She was close to her mother," Terry comforted.

Brad added, "Yeah, and I assure you, whatever her mother told her about you, was not nice. She hated you. I don't mean to be mean or anything, but she did."

"Brad, do not speak ill of the dead. I am sure if the woman

27

hated me, she had her reasons. It is not logical that every person should love me. I'm not always a nice person," Grace rebuked. "I do not blame Wendy for being outraged. It would come as a shock to me, if my father sprung a new wife on me without foreknowledge. I am sure she feels I am stealing her father from her."

"Same ole Grace. Some things never change. New York, huh? What were you two doing in New York? I would never figure Travis the type to go there."

Grace was saved from having to answer. Ruth had sounded the dinner bell. "That is the signal to say supper is on the table. Come, taste the best cooking in the world," but she did not follow. She turned to the comfort of her father figure. "Isaiah, would you make my excuses if I slipped out. I'll probably go to the office or something. I just don't think I need to be here right now. We must give the child time to adjust to the news."

Grace made a call from the phone in the barn for a taxi to pick her up two farms away. She slipped down through the field below the ridge, where she would remain unseen, to cross over into the neighboring pasture. The taxi arrived about fifteen minutes after she did.

The cold office was a welcome to one who had not seen it

for so long. She caught up on all the cases since her leave, until the hour was very late. She checked into a local hotel to rest. Tomorrow, she was scheduled for another radiation treatment. The last thing she needed was the interruption of an angry child. This solitude would do her good. She was not comfortable being sick around other people. Neither did she want to explain her illness to her husband's guests. She would just stay the weekend, and then go home after the girl left. She would not be accused of coming between a father and his daughter.

Grace woke on Saturday, and briefly forgot where she was. Realizing that she must be at the hospital in less than fifteen minutes, she swiftly changed into her clothes. She had left some extras at her office for emergencies. Unfortunately, she only had one pair to change with.

The treatment process lasted around three hours. By the time the actual treatment was completed, the waiting period of recovery, and payment of the bill, Grace was exhausted with a headache. She knew she must start working on Michelle's case, but sickness overcame good senses. She lay on the bathroom floor of her room, too weak to drag her body to the bed, and too sick to leave the commode. She comforted in the fact that she was able to go through this without witnesses. She was far from alone, though. She had her Lord and Savior with her always. Thus, she rested in His comforting arms.

Grace In Time Of Need

The supper conversation was jovial in general. Renee and Terry caught up on the events since the last time they had seen each other. Ruth would join in with a kind word to each of them and begged everyone to help themselves to seconds. There was plenty for all.

Isaiah held his usual quiet demeanor, but was joined this time with the new family member. Travis had not been able to question Isaiah about where and why his wife chose not to come to the table. He knew she had been really sick since Thursday, but surely that had gone by now.

Amy and Michelle explained to Wendy how much fun they would have all together. They laid out plans for all the wonderful things they could do in two days. Wendy forgot she was twenty and began to laugh with the young ones. But Grace never strayed too far from her mind. All the while, her plotting wheels were turning. She would not allow this woman to steal her dad away. She had managed to run her off this time, next time it would be for good.

Travis didn't sleep that night. He waited for his bride to return, but when she didn't, he paced the length of the living room for hours. Isaiah told him privately what Grace had told him, except the part about the office and the part about Wendy. Where could the stubborn woman go? She was ill. She did not need to be by herself right now. Had he known that bringing his family to her home would make her leave, he would never had done so.

Brad woke declaring it to be the best sleep he had experienced in years. None spoke of the weary appearance of their host or the disappearance of their hostess. As a matter of fact, Brad and Terry felt responsible for her having left. Had they known about them getting married, they would have thought differently about coming just now.

After breakfast, Isaiah planted the idea in Travis's head that Grace might be at her radiation treatment. He knew exactly when she had one. He would not forget one session his Lamby would have with that awful mess, but he couldn't betray her confidence. It was not Travis she did not want to deal with, so he felt justified in dropping the hint.

Travis thought hard. Vaguely, he remembered seeing something on the calendar on her desk about it. With a hearty thanks to Isaiah, he confirmed the appointment with her calendar. He excused himself from his guests, except for Terry. He asked her to come with him. He thought he might be able to use her in his search.

Indeed, he caught a glimpse of his wife as she passed the corner of the building. Her strawberry locks would always betray her. He watched momentarily to see if she was going to get in a car or walk. To his denied pleasure, she was walking. There was an inkling in his mind that she might have depended on someone else to help her through this ordeal. A twinge of jealousy had reared up, until he confirmed it not true.

On the way, he had explained to Terry what had happened to his wife. Part of the reason he had wanted her to come, was because of her nursing abilities. Terry's conscience was immediately eased. She felt needed.

They followed the green dress to a hotel only two blocks away, where she disappeared into the mirrored glass doors. Travis found a place to park, and then the duo went to the front desk.

He explained to the clerk that he was Grace's husband and wanted her room number and key. When the clerk eyed Terry curiously, he also showed his license to prove his words were true. She even became more curious when he politely asked her not to ring the room to inform Grace of his arrival.

Twenty minutes later, he finally had the key to her room,

and the two slipped quietly into Grace's darkened hotel room. Terry sat down immediately as if not to intrude in this stranger's personal affairs. Travis searched the room for his lover, when they heard sounds penetrate the closed door of the bathroom.

A more pitiful sight had the man never seen. The all too thin frame of his wife shook in a cold tremble. No more could be expelled from her empty body, yet the stomach's need to heave could not be quenched. A tube of toothpaste lay topless, while Grace leaned pathetically over the tub brushing her teeth. She could not stand even the taste of the paste in her mouth without in sending her to the toilet again. At last, she fell helplessly in a pile on the rug, unable to lift her head.

The husband scooped her up amidst her protests and carried her to bed. She tried to explain to him that she had not the strength to run back to the bathroom when she got sick again. Terry stepped up in her medical capacity. Not much could be done for this, except make the patient as comfortable as possible. Her soft touch caressed Grace's brow with a cool cloth. She sent Travis out to buy some comfortable pajamas for his wife, along with some other necessities.

She cleaned the tub and filled it with warm water. That would have a calming effect on a sick stomach. She disrobed her new cousin and helped her to lie back in the soothing water to relax. It was not long before Grace was feeling better. At least, she no longer desired to turn her body inside out and her head did not seem to ache so hard.

Terry went to the front office to order some hot tea for Grace, but found, surprisingly, that Grace did not like tea at all. "You must drink a little something. The emptiness in your stomach is what is making you so sick. Would you try some Sprite maybe?"

Grace nodded. In only a minute, Terry returned with the soda drink.

Shortly, Travis was offering a pair of gray sweat pants with a white t-shirt. He knew this was what his wife slept in to be the most comfortable, so once more, Terry helped Grace dry off and get dressed. She promptly put her back in the bed where Grace had no problem falling asleep.

The two whispered an argument over who should stay and take care of the sick one. Travis assumed his role as dutiful husband should outweigh Terry's, but in the end, she won out. Her logic that the duty of father came before the duty of husband, therefore, he needed to be home with his daughter. She agreed to have him send Renee to help as well.

Travis tormented over his growing resentment toward

Wendy. She had no right to make Grace feel unwelcome in her own home. Yet, this was his only child. Grace understood the reaction. She had foretold it, before Wendy even came to Oregon. If Grace understood it, then he should as well.

He did not tell anyone where he had been or where Grace was, save Brad. He explained, privately, to Amy and Michelle that Momma would be home in a couple of days, much to their dismay. His wife had chosen not to load this battle for her life on her child. The more she could spare Amy, the better she liked it. Travis need not have told Isaiah and Ruth, for they already suspected.

For The Sake of Grace

Contrary to his better judgment, Travis did not divulge to Wendy about Grace's condition. This was due to Grace's insistence that she did not want Wendy's acceptance out of pity. She must earn it like any other person. On the other hand, Wendy was elated to have run the wicked stepmother out of her own home. This went better than if she had planned it. She thought less of her father's new wife for having been a coward. The least she could have done is pretend to love her dad. How could her father not see the phony he married for what she was?

When Sunday morning rolled around, Wendy refused to go to church. She had won the battle about the wicked stepmother, and she was not going to some stuffy religious meeting to sit for an hour. "I still have dad wrapped around my finger." She thought, but to her alarm, dad was not so easily swayed at this matter. He announced she would be going and that was that. When she told him she had no dresses to wear, he went to his own closet and pulled one of Grace's dresses out and handed it to her.

"I am sure you can wear this." He handed her a dark blue dress.

Wendy eyed the item in admiration. She may not be much,

36

but wicked stepmommy could sure pick out nice clothes. "I am not wearing some old person's dress. I'll see if aunt Renee has something I can wear, if you insist on my going."

Travis's anger was kindled. "Renee is not home. You will not pilfer through her belongings. You will put this on, *now*!" She had never heard him use that tone before.

"Oh Wendy, Momma's dress would look so good on you. I think blue looks pretty on you." Amy came bounding in the room, "Can I sit with you at church?"

Wendy took the dress with a jerk. She could not let Amy know how she hated her mother. "Sure pip squeak. I'll be ready in a minute."

Travis left his daughters to ready themselves for the House of God, while wondering, had Wendy always been this defiant? Why had he never noticed it before? She certainly had her mother's disposition. Oh, how things would have been different, had Grace been Wendy's mother. She would have turned into a beautiful young woman instead of …he could not bring himself to think of her in such a way.

"Brad, I am in a fix between two woman that I love," Travis confided after church was over and the two strolled to the barn. "I know Grace would be angry with me for telling you this, but you are bound to find out sooner or later. Terry already knows. Grace is a very private person, and does not want anyone's pity."

"Well, I can't pity what I don't know," Brad jested in order to lighten his cousin's spirits.

"I just need to talk to someone, and you are the only one I know I can talk to about this. Isaiah and Ruth don't understand. Renee might, but she is not a man, and Grace certainly doesn't understand."

Brad slapped his shoulder, "Your secret is safe with me, Travis."

His laugh became solemn as Travis explained, "Grace has cancer. They found a tumor on her brain. They removed what they could of it, but now she is going through the radiation treatments to get the remainder." Brad listened in silence. "She had a treatment yesterday. That's why she did not come home. She prefers to be private, without prying eyes."

"I understand that. What I don't understand is, why you invited us here, when she was going to be going through all this. The last thing she needed was a house full of intruders."

Travis shook his head. "I thought, and I still think I did the best thing. Terry being a nurse has already come in handy. She and Renee spent the night with her last night, taking care of her. I know she is better today, but she is still very weak. As per her request, I have stayed here with Wendy. Grace insisted I reconnect with my daughter. Does that mean I love Grace less, since I choose Wendy over her? If it does, then I don't deserve her. She deserves first place in my heart, not second."

"What happened to Grace's first husband?" Brad asked.

"I am her first husband. She never married."

Brad frowned, "But Amy's her daughter? Grace never seemed to me to be the type that would…"

Travis interrupted abruptly, "Amy is adopted, Brad. Grace counsels and helps children who have been abused. That is how she came to adopt Amy. Her father was killed, and her mother left her on Grace's doorstep. I am in the process of legally adopting her, as well."

"I beg your pardon. Have you told all this to Wendy?"

"No. Grace doesn't want me to. If Wendy cannot learn to love Grace, because she is a wonderfully incredible person, then she will not love her out of pity. I want to be with my wife, but my wife thinks my daughter needs me more. I have heeded

Grace's wishes. Shouldn't I start heeding to my own?"

"It will all be over today. We catch a plane this afternoon. Then, you can spend all your time with your new bride. She doesn't think you love her less, because you stayed here with Wendy. One thing I know about our old friend is that she is selfless. She meant for you to spend time with Wendy, or she would never have said it. You worry too much."

"I suppose you are right. It's true. Grace wouldn't have done what she did, if she had not intended it with all her heart. I just love her so much that I would not want to treat her less than she deserves."

"Then, by all means, let us go home, and you go bring your bride home."

Travis hesitated, "Can I...at least keep Terry? She can care for her through these treatments."

"She can tell Ruth what to do," he laughed. "Ruth is more than capable of caring for Grace. She has been doing it for years."

Travis went to pick up Terry. He explained to Renee that he was taking them to the airport, and then she could bring Grace on home.

Renee waited for Ruth's call to inform her that the guests were gone, and then Grace paid her bill and left with Renee, like an obedient child.

Healing Grace

The quiet of her house welcomed her tormented head. Ruth provided the patient with her own concocted tea, which was to help Grace's headache to ease. Grace loved the outdoors and her horses; therefore, she refused to lie quietly in her bed. The thoroughbred thrilled in taking the lady of the house on his back to wherever she desired. The fresh air and freedom of the outdoors did more for her, than all the concoctions and beds in the world.

Her strength was still spent, so she could do little physical work. Of course, Isaiah had completed all the chores before she came home. Good old Isaiah always took care of everything.

It was about time for her to go in to ready for church, when she heard the engine of the Mustang in the drive. "Perfect timing!" she spoke to Isaiah. "It has been so long since I have been to church. I miss it terribly." She kissed his cheek and went out of the barn. She was impelled to go to the fence and voice her goodbyes to Samson, but the ringing phone sent her scurrying through the kitchen door and into her office.

As she answered the phone, she politely excused herself to shut the door for privacy. "Mr. Jameston, I have returned."

"Grace, there is a child that needs help that only you can give. Would you be able to get back in the saddle so soon?"

"I am already there."

"Are you sure? Grace, I do not want you to push too hard."

"It'd be the best medicine, Mr. Jameston. It gives me the opportunity to take my mind off of other things."

"Only if you are sure, I have a flight reserved for you in the morning, if you find that you can accommodate me. I know you just got married, but I also realize what these children mean to you. Do you think you can make it?"

This conversation doors continued until it was time to leave for church. None dared to disturb the lady of the house. Amy knew that when the door to the study was closed and occupied, it meant Grace was dealing with business and was not to be disturbed.

"I'm not going to church if she's not going," Wendy said wickedly to her father.

"Grace is going and so are you. We want you here, but you will abide by the rules of this house. This rule states that you will go to church."

43

"I am twenty, Dad. You cannot tell me what to do, and I don't want to go."

Travis smiled at his heathen daughter. "It is my fault that you feel this way, Dear. Had I raised you in church, as you should have been raised, you might have actually found the Lord as your Savior by now. I will always blame myself for that. As for your being twenty, I don't care if you are a hundred, you will come to church as long as you stay in my house."

"You mean her house, don't you dad? She has blinded you into some cult, hasn't she? You have never spoken this way before. Well, that is just fine with me, I'll go home." She had always threatened one parent or the other to manipulate what she wanted, and it had always worked. To her surprise, it didn't work this time.

"Go home if you must, Wendy, but you will go with us to the House of the Lord, as long as you are here. I hope we do not have to have this argument again. Am I clear about that?"

That did it. That woman had hypnotized her dad. He had never dared to speak to her in such a harsh tone before. Neither had he ever defied her in this manner. This made her hate Grace even worse, causing her to try a new tactic.

"What is she doing in there so long? Don't you think you should listen on the other line to find out who she is talking to? I think it is just dreadful that she can find so much to say to another man."

"It is business."

"And just what business is she in that would make her work Sundays?" argued the daughter. If he wanted to play the religious card, that ought to take care of that.

He chose his words carefully. "Her job is twenty-four-seven." He pointed out the conclusion of this conversation, "Amy, are you ready?" He raised his voice to be heard through the closed bedroom door.

Almost immediately, Grace appeared from her study. "Give me two minutes, and I will be in the car." Her words went as quickly as her feet.

Indeed, it was less than two minutes. She changed dresses quickly and ran a brush through her hair while brushing her teeth. She was actually in the Mustang before Amy.

It was then that Wendy decided to wreak her anger to the new stepmother. She had planned how tasteful it would be to see the look of desperation on Grace's face, when she informed her of her intent to stay on in this awful house. Wendy spied the new stepmother's appearance. She hated her all the more. How utterly unfair was it that she could come from the barn and in two minutes look as if she walked off the cover of a magazine? Now was the golden opportunity.

She walked up to the passenger window under the pretense of telling her dad she would be riding with Renee. But, instead of getting the pleasure of seeing Grace squirming in her seat, Wendy was the one squirming. Grace never batted an eye. When she saw Wendy, a gracious smile spread full width across her lips. Not even a twitch could be detected.

"Oh Wendy. I am so glad you decided to stay. I hope you feel at home."

"I could never feel at home in this mausoleum. I would not imagine going *home* without Dad.

"Hopefully, we'll change that. You look so lovely in that red. You must wear that color all the time. It is beautiful on you."

Travis had dreaded about telling his wife about his daughter's decision to stay. He suspected his daughter was up to mischief and wanted to spare Grace any added torment. It pleased him; the refined manner in which his wife accepted the wayward child.

"Anyway, Dad," she emphasized her intent on speaking to her father, not Grace. "I am riding with Renee. Five is too many in this car."

If Grace was relieved of this decision, no one ever knew, save God. She never breathed an unkind word against her husband's child. She never flinched at the ugly words in which Wendy spat forth. She remained unshaken and unmovable.

Redemption's Grace

Unbeknownst to Michelle, she had quite an audience that night. Grace watched the expressions change from moment to moment, as another enlightening truth was revealed from the Word. The dawning revelation that Jesus truly loved her enough to give His own life for her sins impacted her young brain. Slowly, as the story sunk in, a peaceful acceptance spread completely.

Meanwhile, Wendy was watching the same expressions. Of course, she was paying no attention to the words being preached to them. Amazement filled her soul to watch that little waif of a girl. How could a girl that was not living at home with her parents, have a happy peaceful look on her face? She knew if it were her that was taken from home, she would never be happy. Then, there was Amy. Dad said she adopted Amy. Look at the poor kid clinging to Grace, content within her heart to be next to her new mom. Well, this was one person that would not be so easily ensnared in the witch's trap.

When the finale of the service climaxed, the seat next to Wendy became vacant. For Michelle had chosen to make a life altering decision. At the preacher's invitation, the child rose out of her seat and pulled Grace behind. She fairly ran to the altar.

Once she had pulled Grace to her knees beside her, she whispered, "I want to be saved."

Grace prayed swiftly for Guidance. She then quoted the scriptures necessary to show Michelle the way to the cross. She prayed, and then Michelle prayed and asked the Redeemer to save her.

She and Amy talked excitedly on the way home. Grace felt a renewing Strength that came with this new soul for Glory. Soon, she forgot about her illnesses and became light hearted as before. Michelle and Amy both reacted to her gaiety. It had been a long time, since Amy had seen her mother happy.

The following week was busy. Monday morning Grace flew to the Virginia office to counsel a little girl who wouldn't listen to anyone. She almost didn't listen to Grace, but Grace had just the right quality about her that the child needed.

Grace spent two days on the Atlantic coast before returning, only she didn't go home. She was scheduled for another treatment on Thursday. She told her husband ahead of time what her plans were, so he wouldn't worry again.

Thursday and Friday, she spent at the same hotel as before,

recovering from the treatment. She had no intention of exploiting her sickness to her new daughter. Getting away every two or three days would be hard, but she must find a way.

Travis left work on Thursday to attend his wife's treatment. He made sure he was at her side through the whole miserable mess. Afterward, he cared for her through the sickening part as well, thus becoming a routine for them. Each day that Grace had a treatment, he would leave work to be with her. She would hire a room at the hotel for two days. The children became annoyed at mom being gone so much, but only because they loved her.

At the end of the twelfth treatment her hair had thinned a lot, but as for her general appearance, her color returned as she spent many hours in the fresh air. At least the cursed things were over.

She grew stronger physically, but her emotional state would forever be spoiled. There was little distance between God's amazing grace and His incredible mercy, and Grace had slipped through the crack. Due to God's mercy, the emotional scars of childhood had been overcome years prior. Yet, within her weakened state, the hauntings of yesteryear tormented her soul. For her job, this was ultimately dangerous. She could no longer view each victim with total dispassionateness. Now, she wanted to exact punishment upon these perpetrators for their hideous crimes. The objective had since altered its course. The children had become too important. She could feel life slipping from her quickly, and desired to rid the world of evil before she left. She must protect the children, even after she was gone. Yet, she knew not how, and this ate at her soul.

Anger consumed her. Why had she not been more efficient in her work? Why had she not done more, before it was too late? Now, whom could these children depend on? There was no other, save Grace. She needed more time. These were all normal reactions to one finding out they were dying.

The doctor ordered another scan and found the extensions had shrunk only a little. With this knowledge, the battle began to strengthen within her. No longer was she simply fighting this wretched disease; but now, she was discontent with having married a man, that she was going to widow. She was battling with demons for her sanity. And finally, the stubborn woman would not relinquish any of her duties to other helpers. She maintained a full schedule daily, even taking jobs away from Isaiah. She still was frightened for her beloved's health.

Grace and Michelle spent the days together when Grace was able to. She helped with her school, and then the two would do something fun together. Michelle had still kept quiet about the night of the shooting. The advocate knew the girl would confide in her when she was ready.

The only broach to the subject was when Michelle asked one day, "Grace, are you mad at me?"

"No. Why should I be angry with you?"

"I don't know. You haven't asked me about that night. I thought you might be mad."

Grace kissed her brown hair. "You'll tell me when you are ready, Precious."

So that is how they left it.

Grace Supplied

One afternoon, Grace decided to surprise her husband at his work. She had never been to the Sinclair offices in Eugene and had never seen her husband's new office, so she gathered Michelle, and the two drove the short distance to invite him to dinner.

The great beautiful office shone with many shiny windows. It was not nearly as big as Mr. Sinclair's office in New York, but it bore a resemblance to the elite architecture of his New York office. It was only two stories high, but the logo on the sign declared Sinclair's touch of style.

The two huge glass doors at the entrance were heavy. Michelle could not push them open without the aid of Grace's muscle. Grace took in all the busy beings all around them. From the inside, the small two-story building was huge. The outside walls may have been glass, but the inside was beautiful oak. A set of stairs in the wide, open middle was oak as well, varnished to a beautiful dark brown.

On the walls, there hung plaque after plaque of commendations for the company. A circular desk sat in the middle of the first floor. Engraved in the round oak desk was a model of one of Sinclair's planes. Grace stood in awe. Mr. Sinclair did not put on airs of being rich. His humble personality did not match his pocket book.

The woman at the circular desk directed them up the beautiful oak steps. On the second floor, an open balcony overlooked the first floor. The balcony was round, centering the stairs in the middle. Like the downstairs offices, the upstairs offices were adjacent to the outside perimeter.

At the top of the stairs, they looked for the office the secretary pointed out to be Travis's. There was a door with the word 'President', engraved in a gold plate attached to it, on the right side. Across the balcony, directly across from it, was a door marked, 'Vice President'.

Grace did not understand why she was practically having to drag Michelle behind her. Barely off the top step, Grace found her husband talking to a man. It appeared that they were in serious converse, but when Travis saw them, a smile crossed his lips. He nodded his greeting to her.

Grace smiled her charm. He was so handsome. She never imagined Travis Winston would have a job where he would have to wear a suit. Nonetheless, there he stood in black suit, white shirt, and blue tie. He was definitely dashing in a suit.

For some reason, Grace was drawn to look away from her husband to the little girl standing beside her. Her heart skipped when she saw a deathly white Michelle. The eleven-year-old had frozen cold. Her bladder had released the contents uncontrollably. A deathly look came over her. Grace thought the child was having a stroke or something.

Grace To Escape

The frightened look on the girl's face made Grace swiftly react. She stepped in front of Michelle, so that no one could see her. After making sure no one was looking, she quickly swept her into the restroom.

"Michelle, look at me." She patted her cheek. "Honey, look at me. I am going to get you home. Don't be frightened. I will not let anything happen to you. Look at me." She insisted. "Do you trust me?" Michelle forced a nod of her head. "Good, now you wait here and let me get Travis, and then we will sneak out of here."

The child held to Grace's arm trembling. "Don't go, please," she begged in a whisper, which is the only thing she could get to come out of her mouth.

"I'm not going. I will be standing outside this door, and no one will get in. I promise. I'll not be but a minute." She slipped quietly through the door from where Travis had come. She left one hand firmly on the door handle. She deliberately blocked the entrance.

"There you are my beautiful wife," Travis said as she appeared outside the door. "This is a surprise. Are you alone, I thought I saw M…"

Grace shamelessly reached up and kissed his lips to silence him. "Aren't you going to introduce me to your coworker?" She discreetly changed the course of the conversation.

He awkwardly shifted as the kiss slightly embarrassed him. "Um, yes, Grace, this is Ronald Singleton. Ron, my wife, Grace."

The man held his hand out in greeting to Grace. She almost reached for it, but the hair on the back of her neck stood on end. Quickly she retreated any idea of touching him. She smiled slightly, turning back to her husband. "I thought I'd take you to dinner, but I see you are quite busy. Maybe another day. Excuse me." She slipped back into the restroom.

She held a trembling Michelle, until she hoped the boss would have gone back to work and left Travis alone. Explaining to Michelle that she would be right outside the door, Grace opened the door again.

Travis was still standing there, but this time he was alone. "What's going on here, Grace? You were all but rude to my boss."

"We need to get out of here. Do you think you can distract

him? He cannot see Michelle and me leave. I'll explain later. Please, I wouldn't ask if it were not imperative."

Grace was mysterious at times, but he knew the reasons behind it were legitimate. "Give me two minutes. He will be in his office, and then you can get out. You better explain yourself later." He made sure no one was looking, and then lovingly kissed Grace on the head. "I will see you tonight."

Sure enough, in two minutes, Grace and Michelle were able to leave the premises undetected. Michelle said nothing on the way home. Grace did not push her, but she knew the time had come for some explanation.

Grace For A Contrite Spirit

At the house, she put Michelle in the shower and her soiled clothes in the washer. Ruth must have been at the store with Isaiah, for no one seemed to be around.

After she was clean and dry, Michelle approached Grace meekly. Grace prompted after turning on the recorder in her pocket. "You know it is time we got everything out in the open. I cannot help you Michelle, if you don't tell me everything. Why are you afraid of that man Travis was talking to?"

Michelle began slowly, "Dad took me to his work sometimes. I never knew where it was or how to get there. I don't know why. I just don't remember that part."

"That's alright. That is not important right now," Grace urged.

"You know what my dad did to me? Well, that man..." Grace began seeing the picture, and the rage began boiling inside. Michelle continued slowly, as if she found it hard to remember. "It all seems mixed up, like I dreamed it or something, but I know that was the man. I know it. I'm not crazy."

"Honey, you are not crazy. Shall we back up for a minute? Since this all ties in together, tell me what happened the night you shot your dad."

"He came to school with legal papers. He showed them to the schoolmistress. He said he wanted me home, and that he had changed. He hadn't Grace. I could tell. I can't explain it, but I knew."

"I believe you. You do not have to convince me. What happened then?"

"I was so scared. He said you were gone out of town. That scared me even more. So, when he was in the shower, I went to his dresser and got his gun. I knew where he kept it, because I had seen it there when I put his clothes in the drawer. I wasn't going to use it, unless he came in my room. Well, the first two nights, he didn't do anything. He was real nice to me, but that Thursday, he came home acting weird. He yelled at me for taking a bath before he got home. Then, that night he came in. I knew what he was going to do. I waited until he was busy taking his shirt off, and I grabbed the gun from under my pillow. I shot him Grace. I shot him. I didn't really mean to, but I'm glad I did. I hated him." Michelle was on the verge of tears.

Grace enveloped her in her arms, "I know Sweetie. I

understand. We'll have no trouble proving it was self-defense. The recorded history of what he has done to you will prove your innocence. Now, what happened today? You told me that your dad took you to his work sometimes, and that the man Travis was talking to did things to you. Did he do it there at the office? Did it happen more than once?"

"I think so, but I am not sure. I felt kind of funny. Sometimes I would get dizzy and have bad dreams. I am not sure if I was dreaming. I wasn't dreaming the pain afterward."

Grace looked at the eleven-year-old, who suddenly appeared to be thirty. The shame and reproach that child would have to carry for the rest of her life was unthinkable. "Okay, let me ask you this. You already know of the man Travis works with, being involved with what your dad was doing. In your dreams, was any other person involved?"

"I remember two other little girls and a little boy one time. I think there was another man, too. He took pictures, I think." She became frustrated. "I just don't know. I'm sorry."

"You did good, Honey. I hear Ruth in the drive. Will you help her carry in the groceries? I have to go out for a while. Don't worry about any of this. I will take care of it. I will try to make it where you will never have to see that man again."

Grace In Anger

The Irish, red head temper took over the woman's emotion. She thought not of what the best route to take would be. She rode the distance to the Sinclair office building again, seething in anger. Meanwhile, the fury raged within her at the thought of what that beast had done to that poor child, and only God knew how many others. Grace did not think about the recorder still keeping record of each sound, in her pocket. She was not thinking at all.

She entered the beautiful Sinclair building once again. This time, she need not ask for directions. She stormed up the stairs two at a time and went straight into Singleton's office, throwing the door open.

"Mrs. Winston. Why, how in the world are you?" He tried to overlook the fire in her eyes, along with the rude behavior she displayed for the second time today.

She looked different than the picture on his worker's desk. He wondered why it was that she was in the physical shape she was in. He was a calculating man, always looking for future moves in his game. He identified this opponent from the way she barged into his office. He knew her by reputation. She was a force to be reckoned with, or so he had heard. She had been portrayed as a giant, but, seeing her in her physical weakness, he did not fear her.

Grace met him eye to eye. Without giving him the opportunity to stand, she placed her fists upon his desk and fearlessly faced him. "I know what it is you did. Does it make you feel like a man? It is pathetic that a coward like you has to turn to little babies, because you are not man enough to handle a grown woman."

"I'm afraid I don't know what you are talking about, Grace, isn't it?"

"You know of what I speak. It is the treason against human nature in which you have committed so willingly. If you think you are going to get away with it, you have another thought coming."

"I have done nothing wrong for which you can prove," he responded calmly.

"You need not worry about my proof. Be forewarned. I have all the proof I need." She didn't want to jeopardize Michelle by informing him of her witness.

He didn't speak immediately. He stood, still staring into her face, walked over and shut the door quietly. "Grace Sorenson, wasn't it? Yes, I have heard about you. You advocate for those sexually abused children. It's a shame you can't help those children like you think you can. It is a shame about that Bradley girl killing her father, while you were off on a vacation. I can see why you are a suspicious creature," at this point of his answer, his voice became cold and hard. "But don't come in to my office accusing me of something you know nothing of."

"Oh, I know all right. What is more, the judge will know, the community will know, and every person you should dread to know will know. I aim to expose you to the whole world."

"Don't mess with me little girl. I don't know what you think you know, but I am untouchable."

"I know about your whole business of raping these little girls, and hiring them out for the perverted pleasures of others. I *will* bring you down." Grace had only thrown out a wild guess. She had read between the lines of what Michelle had told her, but she baited the fish to see if he would bite.

The man lowered his voice. A hint of fright crossed his face. "You only have guess work. You cannot prove a thing."

"Are you willing to bet your life on it?"

He snarled confidently, "You can't prove a thing. All you

have is scare tactics, and they don't work with me." He realized she knew more than he cared for her to know. He stepped uncomfortably close behind her and whispered in her ear. "Before I'm through with you, you will beg me to hurt you."

She wheeled to face him. "I am not afraid of you. I am not a child that can be intimidated by your idle threats," she spat.

"I make no idle threats, little girl," he still spoke quietly.

"Your threats are as idle as your brain. You have been warned." She did not wait for a response. She turned to leave.

"Oh Grace. How is your newly adopted daughter doing? Is she getting along with the Bradley girl?" He threw behind her in sugary sweet words.

This only infuriated the red head more. She flung the door open and walked right into Travis's chest. She did not even stop to apologize.

Grace Under Fire

He had seen Grace go into Singleton's office when he was on the phone. He finished his call, and then went to investigate why his wife was behind closed doors with a man she did not even know.

He watched in bewilderment as his wife descended the stairs to the front door. He turned to Singleton, but before he could say a word, Singleton spoke. "Winston, you're fired. Get your stuff and get out. If you are still on these premises in ten minutes, I will have you arrested.

"Ron, you did not hire me; therefore, you cannot fire me. If you have a problem with my work, then I suggest you take it up with Mr. Sinclair." He knew not what had transpired between his wife and boss, but he was not going to side with the enemy.

"Very well. I will talk to Sinclair about it."

Singleton stormed into his office and slammed the door. He called down to the security gate. "The woman that just left out of here in the blue four door is not to be on these premises again. If she comes back, have her arrested immediately."

Several other secretive calls were made behind his closed

door, while Travis sat at his desk trying to fathom what had transpired in that office. He still had forty-five minutes until five o'clock. He could hardly wait to talk to Grace.

As he drove home from work, he noticed a black car, which seemed out of place for an old country road, follow him to his drive. It slowed for a minute then proceeded on. Travis did not ordinarily take much notice of things being out of the ordinary.

Grace was not home, much to his aggravation. Confound her! He wanted to find out what was going on. Amy welcomed her new dad by jumping into his arms and telling him about her day at school, while Wendy remained seated on the couch. Michelle and Ruth were concocting a delicious smelling feast in the kitchen. Of course, Isaiah was out in the barn, and Renee had not come in from work.

Renee came home around six and reported Grace had not come in to the office all day. Travis hoped she had been at the office all evening. His spirits sank.

To make matters worse, there appeared to be a huge storm blowing in from the coast. It was supposed to rain into the early hours of the morning, and then turn to snow. Surely Grace would have enough sense to not take off unannounced, knowing he would be worried. Michelle had been quiet all evening, with a sad worried look of her own. Travis did not have the heart to question her about his wife, or the events of the day. "Keep her safe, Lord, keep her safe," he prayed.

Grace on the Run

Grace spent the remainder of the afternoon at the courthouse, scrutinizing the documentation involving Michelle's situation. She brought out the paper, which Bradley had shown to the school's mistress, in order to bring her home again. Judge Harris was the judge that signed the release. Now, why did that not surprise her? It seemed Harris had his dirty paws in this case all along.

Grace was left alone in the records room around four thirty, yet she could not shake the feeling of evil eyes bearing through her back. She tried several times to immerse herself back into the paper work, but to no avail. She could not help feeling that someone was watching her. She discreetly looked around yet saw no one. Finally, realizing she was not accomplishing anything, she decided to leave.

She went by her office to ensure Renee was safely gone for the day. Grace was soon lost in trying to figure all the players of the game and their positions. It was nearly six o'clock when she took leave of her office.

The sky had darkened, causing an early nightfall. Dark clouds had gathered to open their force and pour rain upon the earth below. Grace relocked the office behind her and ran to her car. The old blue four door was Ruth and Isaiah's, but since Travis had moved in, Grace started using it.

Grace was almost home. A seven-mile road lay between the inhabitants of town and the desolation of the farms, where Grace resided. This particular road had only a few homes at the beginning and end of it. In between, there lay fields for planting mostly corn and a river deep within its banks. During the harvesting season, one could not see any distance for the tall stalks of corn that blanketed each side of the road after the river.

Bright headlights suddenly rounded the curve ahead, causing Grace to shield her eyes. She was going to slow down until the car passed, but she could see another car in her rear view mirror. It was coming fast. Did it not see the bright lights ahead? It better slow down. Surely it was not going to pass her.

Before she could think, the car behind had bumped and jolted her car beyond her steering ability. The headlights in front were getting closer. They seemed to be in her lane. She could not swerve without running over the steep embankment of the river's edge. She had no time for thought. The car, or it seemed a bigger vehicle than a car, had rammed her again. This time, the oncoming car had impacted her front corner, sending her front end over the side of the river.

70

Grace's car was nestled in the limbs of the trees that grew out of the side of the river. She could hear the snapping of the branched beneath the weight of her car. Quickly, she opened her door to get out. The two other vehicles could be heard speeding out of sight, after waiting together for a few minutes. She had barely wrapped her tired arms around the tree when the last holding limb snapped with a deafening sound. The sound had been magnified in her fright. The car fell with a splash and crash.

The torrent of rain made climbing down the tree near impossible. Her dress was ripping on limbs as she passed them slowly. At one point, her hands slipped, causing her to fall a few feet, before she could grab a hold of another branch. This caused an excruciating pain in her arm.

The dark icy waters roared mightily beneath her. They were as a large giant, waiting for her to fall into the open mouth for consumption. She was too cold and frightened to move fast or pray hard. Branch by painful branch, she made her way to the bottom, where the waters were almost deafening. They had swollen almost to the heights of their banks from the sudden amount of rain poured out from heaven. At long last, she was on the bottom limb. Her feet dangled, aiming for a foothold on solid ground. All she could find was a soft piece under the rim of the water, where a tree was rooted, giving her a place to stop from sliding.

The cold water was not a shock for her limbs. She was already numb. Her fingers, hands, toes, and feet held no feeling in them whatsoever. She inched her way back over the top of the edge to solid earth. At the top, she looked both ways to see if help could be around the bend. This road was deserted most of the time in good weather. Why should anyone be out on a night like this, if they did not have to be?

Headlights appeared from the direction she had just come. "Thank you, Lord." She uttered, while stumbling to the edge of the pavement. She threw her arms into the air to the best of her frozen ability. Hot tears burned, and the cold raindrops froze her face. Help was here just when she needed it.

The car slowed down a short distance from where Grace was standing. Surely, they could see her silhouette in the headlights. She waited for someone to emerge and offer her help. Help did not come. In fact, no one emerged from the car. Instead of help, the car's engine raced, and squealing tires spiraled the vehicle straight toward her. They could not have lost control from a dead standstill. This was intentional! Grace stepped back from the road, lest she should not be seen and hit. She still wanted to believe it was someone trying to help her. Yet, the headlights followed her off the shoulder. Further she went.

Further the headlights went. The car was heading straight for her!

Grace dove over the bank where the car could not follow. Her face was stricken with the icy waters that had earlier beckoned to her. She lay silent and still, soaking in the river, and praying that she would not be seen in the headlights, that were now searching over the river. She dared not even breathe.

There was a loud thud of metal hitting something and then a hiss. The car hesitated for what seemed an eternity, and then puttered away like a wounded dog. Even after the last sounds of the engine faded away, Grace dared not move, except to inch her way out of the water line. She lay for a long time in the brambles of the bank, listening to an occasional engine pass by. None stopped or even slowed, since the one that aimed for her. All thoughts were lost in the freezing rain. "Help me, Father," was all she could manage to pray.

After what seemed to be an eternity, she was given the Peace within that it was safe to proceed. She slowly, because of the aching, freezing muscles, pulled her tiny frame over the top of the embankment again. There was no sign of life around. True darkness of the night had fallen around her. She was alone, wet and shivering, freezing, and possibly dying in the dark night.

Grace tried to put one foot in front of the other. If she could stay active, she could possibly make it. She had no doubt that hypothermia had already taken her. It was a little over three more miles to her house. If she could hold out that long, she would be all right. Her prayers were brief and incoherent at times, but the Advocate understood each one. She could not think very clearly. Thirty minutes had passed, but in the cold, biting wind and rain, to her it seemed days. The rain had lessened a little, and had Grace looked up, she would have realized that the rain was no longer. It was snowing!

Grace's face was hidden in her chest with folded arms trying to keep her warm, but she could see the oncoming lights of another vehicle behind her. She did not care. If they were going to run her over, then so be it. She had no more strength left in her to run or fight anymore. She would make it easy for them. She would lie down in the middle of the road for them to have an easier target. Actually, she would fall into the road, for her legs and feet were numb with cold and could no longer be used.

Once again, the beams targeted her out. "I guess it is my time," she thought vaguely. The engine slowed down, finally coming to a halt. "I suppose they are going to make sure they finish me off once and for all."

Rescuing Grace

Travis had eaten little at the supper table. He had an uneasiness about his wife that he could not put a finger on. He could not very well share his feelings with anyone else. They would have thought him a fool and laughed. Everyone knew how Grace would disappear inexplicably. Somehow, this was different. He couldn't explain the uneasy nudging that she was in trouble.

After supper, he went to the barn to complete her tasks there. Samson snorted and kicked as if he, too, knew something was wrong. If only Samson could understand him, then he would have someone to confide in. He shared with the magnificent beast his fears, but was given no consolation from one that could not return verbalization.

He came to the conclusion that he was going in search of his wife. He implored the aid of his sister, and they set out after eight o'clock to find her. The rain had pounded the earth for over two hours, with no hope in sight for it to slack. They took the candy apple red Mustang and began the search. They planned to stop periodically to call home to check if she had returned.

They went first to the hotel room in which Grace would stay

during her treatments. The clerk had not seen her all day. That was a dead end.

Another failed mission was the trip to the office. Renee informed him that Grace must have been at the office at some point after she left, because Grace's door was open, and Renee specifically closed it. She mentioned to her brother that Grace's office had frightened her. Grace's desk seemed upset compared to the usual. Through all this evidence, there was no sign of what hour she might have vacated it.

Renee had the idea to call Stephanie, while they were at the office. She made her call, while Travis called the house, but no news came from the home front. Ruth tried to hide her concern, but since her soul mate had showed signs of being restless and worried, she became so too. Isaiah was not one to give in to worrying over Grace's whims or disappearances. Usually, if the Irish free spirit vanished, it was to deflect the bad guys from the house in order to keep the children safe. Under normal circumstances, she would touch base with someone and let them know she was safe by now. The fact that she had not called or had not been seen by anyone for so long began to concern him. The longer she went without contacting them, the more worried he and Ruth became.

Stephanie reported having seen Grace at the courthouse

earlier, but she could not be sure if she saw her leave. She also reported that Grace seemed agitated.

"Where do we go from here?" Travis asked of his sister, when they were on the road once again.

"Tell me again, what exactly happened at work today?"

"She and Michelle came at dinner, but they left before we could go. Grace said she would explain when I came got home. They were both acting weird. As a matter of fact, when I reached where they were standing, Michelle was in the restroom, and Grace had just come out. I introduced her to my boss, and Grace was kind of rude to him. Then, they left. About an hour and a half later, I saw Grace go into my boss's office. I was on the phone, so when I hung up, I went to see what was going on."

Renee frowned, "She didn't come to see you at all?"

"I'm not sure. When she came out of Ron's office, she barreled into me without a word and left. I don't even know if she realized it was me. It happened so fast."

"That certainly doesn't sound like Grace. Maybe we should question this Ron guy that she was talking to. He may know what upset her."

Travis hesitated, "I don't think that would be a good idea. After Grace left, he tried to fire me."

"He did?" The sister could not believe her ears. "What did you do?"

"I told him that he didn't hire me, and he couldn't fire me. Only Mr. Sinclair has that power. He was not happy about it, but he had no choice."

"Ooh, it sounds like Grace put a bee in his bonnet. I wonder what it could be about. I suppose one doesn't make a lot of friends in this business, but that doesn't help us with our present predicament, now does it?"

"I doubt it. I mean, what could the president of an airline company have to do with a child advocate for sexually abused children. He's not even married, and I certainly do not think he has any children. I have never seen any pictures of them, anyway."

"So we're back to square one." she sighed.

"I suppose we go home, get on the wire, and call everyone we can imagine that would know where she might be. That is all I know to do."

Renee comforted, "I guess you are right. I met a private investigator in the office today. He came by offering his service as a freelancer. He said he couldn't afford to do it for free, but he would love to help out the little kids. I could call him. He might have more luck than us in finding her."

"Private eye, huh? I reckon it's not good when you need an investigator keep up with your wife." He tried to alleviate his fears. "Renee," he squinted his eyes, looking ahead, "is that a person walking in this storm?"

Renee looked carefully. "Why, I believe it is. Travis, someone is out in this wet mess. They may need help. It is cold tonight. The rain is mixed with snow."

Travis slowed. "Renee, that is Grace!"

"She looks wet. Pull over, quick!"

The car had barely stopped when Travis jumped from it with a leap. "Grace! Grace!"

The woman could not turn her head to the voice calling her. Instead, her legs finally gave way at the sound of her husband's voice, and then she collapsed to her knees without feeling.

Travis scooped her up. "Renee, you drive. Hurry. We need

to go back to town. She needs the hospital."

He unbuttoned his shirt and tucked her arms around his warm body. She was cold as ice. He took his face and lips and held them close to her face, switching sides periodically. He wrapped her legs and feet in his and Renee's coats after removing the wet shoes.

Grace lay in the warmth of her husband's bosom; however, she could not move her frozen lips to respond to his question. The heat of the car pierced her body with burning spears. She was completely numb from head to toe. All she could feel was the pain of her body warming.

Discovering Grace

The hospital immediately submerged her in a pool of warm water. This was painful but necessary. Grace was fighting with every breath to say something, but her brain did not seem to function under her control. When she was once again able to control her tongue, she pleaded with her husband.

"Michelle, you must protect her. Go keep her safe."

He gently touched her cheek. "Michelle is fine. She is with Ruth and Isaiah. Nothing is going to happen to her. Stop worrying."

"Please," she begged, "tell Ruth code green. She is not safe. Go! Now!"

"Are you sure?" Her husband asked in concern.

"I have to call Ruth. Michelle…"

"I will call Ruth, but you must promise to stay right here."

"Tell her code green," she called after him.

When Travis called the house, no one answered the line at

all. He called three times to ensure he had dialed the right number, and then had Renee call it as well. He was not happy with this response. He should not have to go back with this report to his wife.

True to character, Grace did not accept this. Most of her body had regained the feeling, albeit the feeling of stinging pain. Travis knew how important it was for her to get home. Did this mean that Amy was in danger, too?

She feared what Singleton had done to her loved ones. He made it clear by running her off the road tonight, that he would stop at nothing to keep the truth from coming out. Yes, she was convinced that it was none other than Singleton. The timing was too exact. This meant that he would be trying to silence Michelle. With his sadistic way of thinking, the only way to do that may be to get rid of Michelle. Grace prayed a special prayer for Michelle's safety and then for the others.

Travis gave her his coat, so the skin would not freeze again. That was more dangerous than getting frostbite in the first place. He shielded her from the snow, which had since started accumulating.

Once they were settled in the back seat of the Mustang, and Renee at the driver's seat, Travis demanded to know what had happened. He was not going to wait for anything else to happen before he found out what was going on with his wife.

Grace explained how the criminal acts of Travis's boss had been revealed to her. She admitted to having let her anger get the best of her when she went to the office to tell him off. She explained to him about being run off the road by two vehicles, one coming and one going. She told about the car coming back to make sure she was incapacitated.

"I had it all on tape, but I am afraid it was damaged in the water and rain. I will try to salvage what I can, but I hold no hope. Let's pray he did not get his hands on Michelle. He is desperate enough to hurt anyone in his way. At least we know he had one other cohort, because it was two cars that ran me off the road, not one."

"So, do they think you are out of the picture?" Renee asked from the front.

"I don't know what they are thinking. What I do know is, most of my guesswork today must have hit the nail on the head, or they would not be so threatened."

Travis didn't say much. His mind was racing about what had happened to Grace and possibly his children. What could be done? What should be done now?

"I knew something was up; although I had no idea of how serious. When you came out of his office, Ron was so angry, he fired me."

"He did?"

"Of course I told him that he had no power to fire me. He wasn't too happy, but he had no other choice."

Grace spoke while deep in thought. "That's good. I would like to have someone watching him that I can trust. Can you be my eyes and ears on the inside? I need to contact Mr. Sinclair. He'll not be too happy to find he has such criminals working for him. How could I do that? I would be afraid to call him. There is no telling who might be listening on the line. No, I must do this in person. Has anyone else noticed the headlights that seem to have been following us since we left the hospital? If someone is watching us, then I can't let anyone know I am going to New York. It would not prove good to tip my hand." She continued talking, more to herself than to anyone else, without giving anyone the chance to respond. Her brain just kept throwing questions and suggestions out like a machine.

Travis held his finger to her lips. "Slow down. First of all, yes I noticed the car behind us. I wasn't sure, but since you noticed it as well, I am convinced that it is following us. We are almost home. We will see what happens when we turn in the drive. Second, you cannot fly to New York. It would do you no good. Mr. Sinclair is in California. He is to be there for the better part of next week. Thirdly, there is no 'I' going anywhere. If you insist on going, you *will* go with me. This sounds too dangerous for you to handle alone. For crying out loud, they tried to kill you tonight. Do you honestly think I would let you go alone?"

Renee watched her brother through the mirror. She could not see much in the dark, but if he could read her thoughts, he would have gotten an eye full. She would never allow anyone, especially a man, to 'let' her do anything. Her brother shouldn't speak to Grace that way. Then, Renee got the surprise.

Instead of reacting as Renee would have done, Grace spoke calmly with admiration in her eyes. "Of course, you're right. I was not thinking clearly. If he is in California, we could make the drive tonight. We could be there before the morning light breaks."

"I do not think you are in any condition to go anywhere tonight," the husband protested.

"Nonsense. It's not very far. We don't rightly have a choice. I mean to bring this man to justice, along with any others involved in this crime." They were pulling into the drive. "Renee, will you stop here. I would like to shut the gate and set the alarm."

"I will. What part of, 'you are not doing anything', did you not understand?" Travis demanded. "You heard what the doctor said. You cannot get too cold at all."

The car was still behind them when they turned off, but it continued out of sight down the road. After a few minutes, when Travis had completed shutting the gate, Grace saw a pair of lights coming in the opposite direction, as they passed the bend in the drive.

Securing Grace

No one was in sight upon arrival. The house was deathly quiet. It had an air of pall upon it. Renee shuddered at the coldness it permeated.

"I don't understand," the sister said, "where is everyone? They were here when we left."

"It is alright, Renee." Grace comforted. "They're safe." Renee looked confused. "Someone needs to check the perimeters of the property and pretty much every square inch. Since I was voted out of doing anything worthwhile, that means one of you two must do it, my dear husband," she smiled mischievously.

He laughed, "Me? Why do I get the pleasure?"

"Because you are the man of the house. Surely you would not let your sister ride in the dark looking for bad characters, would you?"

"I guess not." He slumped in mock disappointment. "The things you gotta do when you are the only guy."

Grace called after him, "Take Samson. If you have not returned within thirty minutes, we'll come looking for you.

Come on Renee, let's check your apartment."

Renee and Grace completed the indoor search first. Grace went ahead and showered and put a clean change of clothes on while waiting on her husband. Meanwhile, Renee sat alone in the living room, letting every sound and shadow take advantage of her imagination.

"I feel a hundred percent better," Grace stated coming out of the bedroom. Has Travis not yet come back?" She peered out the window.

"I thought I heard him on the porch a minute ago."

Grace opened the door to the stomping of snow from boots. "Any sign of anything unusual?"

He reported, "Nope. All fences are in tact. It would take a lot to get on this property unnoticed. Now what?"

"Would you like to clean up, before we go?"

While he was showering, Grace led Renee to her study to open the hidden door behind the fireplace. Renee stood in awe.

"I never knew it did that. Wow! What's behind it?"

"Come, you will see." Grace took her through the small

doorway and into a dark hall. "Ruth!" called Grace, "Isaiah! Is everyone safe?"

"In here, Lamby."

Renee stood in astonishment at the apartment in which she stood. It was perfect. One of the two bedrooms off to the right held two sleeping bodies. Wendy, who had refused to go to sleep until she found out her dad was safe, was in a comfortable chair in what looked like a den. Isaiah was in the other bedroom with the door closed. Grace explained the routine to Renee in case the occasion ever arose for the need.

Renee still stood in amazement. She had no idea this space ever could have existed. "Wow! You can live somewhere for months and never know where you live.

"What possessed you guys to come down?" Grace asked after explaining the events of the night in limited version.

"Soom man knocked on the door. He seemed a mite soospicous, so I hid the wee oons and waited till he looked in the windows for a bit and left. Isaiah was in the barn. I fetched him quick like and told him to lock the gate. It had been a while since we had heard froom you Lamby."

"You did wonderful. That is why I love you all so dearly.

You have a good head on your shoulders, Ruth." She turned to Wendy and spoke quietly, while Renee and Ruth conversed. "Please understand. This place has to be kept completely secret. I am in no position to tell you what to do, but I adjure with your sense of decency. These girl's lives are in danger. If anyone ever found out about this room, they could be hurt or even killed. It is not me these men are after. They want Michelle. So I ask you with utmost sincerity, please do not ever tell a living soul about this place."

The girl's only answer was an angry scowl. Of course, she would never do anything to jeopardize either one of them. She really felt close to them, but she was not about to be nice to Grace. Let step-mommy suffer and wonder if she was going to turn her in or not.

Grace felt it necessary for them to remain here for at least another night, much to Wendy's chagrin. She was not happy until her dad came through the darkened hall. She ran to him with a huge hug in hopes of making Grace jealous, but Grace did not seem to notice. "Drat it all! What would it take to make this woman mad?" She asked herself.

They all agreed that until Grace could find a way to inform Singleton and return unseen, the rest of the gang needed to stay in the shelter. Renee was the least happy about this decision.

She had just met this private investigator, and they were supposed to go out next evening. Grace appeased her by assuring her she would do all in her power to be back in time for Renee to keep the date.

Plan of Grace

By the moonlight, Travis and Grace drove quietly from their home. Grace lay in the back floor to hide from any prying eyes. It would look as if a single driver were in the car. The utmost care was taken in ensuring secrecy.

The looming dark form, which appeared to be a car, was still at the end of the second driveway from theirs. Travis turned onto the main road, while his wife remained unseen. Sure enough, several miles down the long road, where Grace had met her challenge only hours earlier, headlights were seen in the distance behind them.

On the outskirts of town, the car seemed to be sticking with following them. Travis drove in the northern direction. He aimed to throw his pursuers into another direction. Grace was still hidden. As the passing lights from the small towns crossed the red Mustang, only one body was in sight.

He pulled into a well-lit gas station. He paid for the gas first, and then hurried back to fill the tank. When a car pulled up on the other side to buy gas as well, the man inside imposed to ask of Travis directions to some place he had never heard of. The man nonchalantly looked into the Mustang.

"What kind of engine does she have?" The stranger asked to cover his truthful purpose of looking inside. He spoke with Travis about the car for a few minutes, and then left to pay.

This was Travis's opportunity to lose him. He quickly hopped in the car and headed onto the road again, going north. As soon as he was out of sight of the station, he hung a right, turned his lights off, and made another immediate right onto a back street. He coasted to the end of the block to watch for the other car to pass. When after a minute or two, he shot through the intersection, and then the next one that ran behind the gas station. He passed each intersection quickly. This is the way he backtracked through the town. He would have to take the back roads to a certain point, or else be found out.

Two and a half hours later, they were able to emerge onto Interstate 5. Grace no longer was on the back floor. She had moved up to a more comfortable position in the seat. Every time headlights came behind them, Travis grew nervous, hoping and praying it was not the dreaded car.

It was not until the Mustang pulled in front of the hotel where Mr. Sinclair was registered, nine hours from their departure that Grace dared to rise up from her hiding. They hadn't stopped to call the boss for lack of time and the urgent need for secrecy. It was in the early rays of the new day when they knocked on Mr. Sinclair's door.

It was a tremendous surprise to the man to see his two favorite people standing at his Californian hotel door, but the bigger shock came when Grace told of the reason they had come. He sat patiently waiting for her to finish telling of yesterday's events. He thought for a while silently. This attribute of always thinking things through before acting upon them is what made him such a good businessman. He never did anything off the wall.

"I had wondered at the passing of Bradley. I heard the circumstances surrounding his death, but I had no proof of any foul play," he told them at last. "About Singleton, I want you to keep your eye out Travis, and Grace I want you to stay away from him. He is not too fond of you. We want to keep you alive for a while longer."

"I shall heed those words, Mr. Sinclair."

"Good. Grace, you stay away from him. Travis, watch him without raising suspicion. If he gets too friendly or suspicious acting, then let him fire you. We'll take it one day at a time. I will work from my end while waiting to get some feedback from you. Thank you for letting me know. It chaps my hide to think I have a cretin like that on my payroll. Go home and be safe.

Farewell, my friends. May God be with you."

Grace smiled at the farewell words of Mr. Sinclair. Maybe the Lord was working on his heart as well. It would be wonderful if the Sinclairs would all come to know Him as a personal Savior. Catholicism was a completely different belief than that of the Word of God. They defied the Word in many ways. For one, they believe in confessing to a man for forgiveness. No one can give redemption save the One who died for those sins we are confessing. It is through His blood we are forgiven, and those sins are washed away, never to be remembered anymore.

Grace For A Frame Up

Travis and Grace drove to the outskirts of Springfield, before Grace hid on the back floorboard. The late afternoon was dreary with gray skies hovering beneath any remnants of sunshine. A watchful eye could not spot any discrepancies in the number of riders in the red Mustang.

As they started down the long lonely stretch of road where Grace had been run off, a blue light began whirling on its axis in the rear view mirror. "We have company." Travis said without turning his head. "I was not speeding. I don't know what they want."

Grace pulled the coat on the seat over her. When the officer came to the window, he asked Travis to step out. Grace took this opportunity, when he was distracted, to quietly open the rear door and slide out. She lifted the handle and pressed the door tightly before letting it go. She crawled on hands and knees to a nearby tree, where she hid from view.

She could hear parts of the conversation. "...to check your car. I had a call from someone that you are carrying illegal substance. If you don't mind, I'll ask you to open your trunk and stand back."

The officer watched the suspect for possible rebellion, but when the search was complete, nothing had been found. The officer came to the back door and opened it. Travis held his breath. What if he was really searching for Grace?

"I'll declare," started the officer. "I don't know what the caller was insinuating, but I see nothing suspicious here. Where are you heading?"

Travis let his breath out in a surprised relief. "Home. I have been out of town. As you can see by my unshaven face, I have had a long night."

"Well, by all means, head home. I apologize for bothering you. Do you have much further to go? Where do you live?"

"At the Sorenson farm."

"You must be Grace's new husband. I don't know why I didn't recognize her car sooner. There are not two of these babies around here. Again, I apologize."

"No apologies necessary. It was no problem."

He raised his voice as he departed to his own car, "Give my love to Grace and Ruth."

"Will do," Travis waved goodbye.

He peered into the back seat, where the officer had moved the coats that were once piled in the floor to the seat. There was no Grace! He could not very well look for her without raising suspicion. "Where in the world did she disappear to this time?" he wondered.

He had to drive on, while the officer remained parked long enough to call in his search. Travis could still see the black and white vehicle as he rounded the bend.

Grace For Every Mile

Meanwhile, Grace inched her way, crawling on her belly, over the embankment of the swollen river through the snow. Just enough room remained for her tiny body, before the water would have overflowed her banks. She heard the engine of the first vehicle, and still she waited patiently. She did not want to risk being seen, just in case it was the officer that was remaining. It was after the second engine faded in the direction in which it came that she dared raise her head. Before she could top the rise, though, she heard the engine of a third car. It passed without slowing down. She lifted her head, once more, to make sure the coast was clear. The third passing car was a black car. She could hardly see it. By the time she lifted up, it was rounding the bend.

"Was it a black car that hit her from the front yesterday?" she asked herself. She could not see the one behind, but as she was being pushed sideways, the headlights of the car behind were exposing the car in the front. She had little time for scrutiny, but she was sure it was black.

She made her way across the blacktop and ran hastily across the open field to the bordering tree line. She worked her way toward her own farm slowly, cautiously. Quick were her steps, scarcely touching the ground at all. Grace could feel her illness and age. She was not as spry as she used to be. Now, she wore out much quicker. Now, she was forced to make frequent resting stops.

Eventually she made the crossing to her own land via river. The old fishing hole was a sight for sore eyes. She had to cross over the road one more time before reaching this point, but at last, she was home. She knew her way around these woods quite well. In the years past, she had traipsed all through them while hunting with Isaiah. She knew how to cross her perimeters unnoticed and without setting off the alarm. None would dream of coming all this way to find a hole in the system. Actually, she must find a way to fix this hole. In order to fence it, she would have to run the electric fence through the river, which would be impossible to do. The urgency of getting that problem solved was growing each day.

At last! She was home. Samson came trotting through the darkness for his mistress. He gladly carried her wet body to the barn. It was still cold, but she had little time to freeze between the fishing hole and barn when riding on Samson. He accepted her pats and hugs, before she left him.

The Mustang was not in sight. Travis must be out looking for her. Oh well, there was nothing she could do about that now. She showered in hot water, letting it soothe her weariness. She started a fire in the fireplace, called Travis on the car phone, got no answer, so she waited for her husband to return.

She tried to play the wet tape without success. The words were few and far between, and pretty much garbled on top of that. It was hopeless. No judge would take this as acceptable evidence, when you couldn't even tell who was on the tape.

Before long, her tired eyes refused to stay open any longer. Her exhaustion from the last twenty-four hours had caught up with her. She slept hard, dreaming of Singleton and some other goon chasing her and Michelle through some strange woods. They were lost. They seemed to be running around in circles, without any knowledge of how to escape. Michelle had run until her legs gave out. Grace was forced to carry her. Slower, they ran, and then, even slower, until she could see Singleton. He carried a hunting rifle propped upon his shoulder. Once within range, he raised his gun, with a resounding snap, Michelle's small body went limp in Grace's arms.

"No!" she cried out. "Michelle, listen to me. Hold on. Hold on."

Her cries became murmurings, "No. Don't touch her." Somehow, he and his goons were now carrying Michelle away.

He was laughing at Grace and waving. "Michelle!" With that scream she bolted into consciousness.

She lay still, with her eyes closed because she felt someone leaning over her. She could hear his breath. She was about to roll over with a punch in the nose, when she heard, "Grace. Wake up. Honey, wake up. Grace."

She rolled over with a punch to his arm. "You startled me. When did you get home?"

"Just now. When did you get home?" asked her husband.

"A while ago. I didn't dare come in search for you."

"Well, that is where I have been, in search of you. Where did you disappear to?"

Grace yawned, "That is a story for another day. Right now, let's ready for bed. I am exhausted. It has been a long day. If you want to shower, I can rustle up some supper."

"Sounds good to me. I am starved." He drew his wife in his arms. She was so precious to him. He couldn't bear the thought of something happening to her. "I am glad you are safe at home, dear."

"I am glad we are all safe at home. Singleton wants
102

Michelle out of the picture before her court date. I'm not sure why they have not set it yet, but it cannot be too far away. I am sure her testimony threatens him."

"We can keep her safe. It is our job as parents. Nothing can come between the love of a parent for their child." Grace smiled at him softly. He added, "What are you looking at me that way for?"

"You are talking as if she were your daughter. Have you been having the same thoughts about that child as I have?"

"Oh Grace. She has lived with us for most of our married life. This farm would be so empty without her. Amy loves her. How will it affect our Amy for Michelle to leave?"

"How will it affect Amy's dad? I believe it is unanimous. We shouldn't tell her until this whole mess is over. Once her court appearance is over, and she is no longer thinking of how to stay alive, we'll celebrate. I do love her." She kissed her lover softly. "She and I have something in common. We both lost our mothers at a very young age. I can relate to that. She has no one. Stephanie tried to locate any kind of family, but she has none."

Protective Grace

Grace and Travis decided that they would not live in fear of the devil. The family would not forego church on the Lord's Day for any reason, if possible. They planned to take special caution with the girls. Other than that, they refused to let anything be different.

All the adults lectured Michelle and Amy about never talking to strangers, let alone getting in a vehicle with anyone other than those that lived on the farm. Utmost caution must be taken. Amy and Travis didn't understand why Grace was so adamant about protecting Amy, when it was Michelle they were after. Grace deliberately kept silent about Singleton's veiled threat against the daughter.

From that moment on, they became overprotective to the girls. All overnight slumber parties were tabooed. Grace made sure someone took Amy to and from school, while Michelle began an intense regime for catching up her schoolwork to grade level. Grace intended to make this a normal functioning family, before it was over. There was to be no idle time for thoughts of wicked evil men, but each was fully aware of the lurking vehicles and spying eyes that followed them wherever they went.

They all prepared for the excitingly expectant weeklong visit from Brad and Terry for the Easter holiday, per their arrangements. Grace was more excited about the visit this time. She would not have to be embarrassed by some treatment or sickness, because she was mending nicely. She would be more prepared for visitors this time.

Amy was most excited about their coming. She had developed a huge crush on Brad. He had shown her and Michelle a lot of special attention the last time. Terry and Brad only had Stacy, but the way Brad loved children, he should have had a dozen. Anyway, he loved to spoil them all.

The only one who was not excited about their coming was Wendy. She knew that they would put a dent in her plans to split up her dad and stepmother. They knew her too well.

However, it did not take Brad and Terry to stall her plans. Wendy was finding it harder to hate her mother's opposition as each day passed. Grace gave no interference in Travis and Wendy's relationship. She treated Wendy as the adult that she was, and Wendy appreciated it, because Grace was the only one that treated her as such. To her dad and aunt, she would always be their little girl. Grace had a quality about her that few people possessed. Her natural charm and kind heart refused to allow anyone that really knew her to hate her. Besides, she was not the one constantly nagging her to get up and do something around this God-forsaken farm. Her dad forbade her to lie around all day and watch Ruth work her fingers to the bone. Despite her pleasure, Wendy was becoming quite a homemaker.

Graceful Endeavors

Grace was in Oklahoma when the cousins arrived. She had been called on business to help start another branch of the Jameston organization. Jameston had not halted his plans to expand, because of Grace's illness. In fact, he had elected to begin more foundations at several other locations. The only difference was that he was doing the footwork in lieu of his best worker. He had everything in order, down to the applicants lined up for interviewing. He did not trust his own judgment, when it came to picking out a suitable counselor for the many children that were sure to pass through these doors. Grace would have better knowledge of the qualifications for the person who would be in charge of so many crucial effects.

Albert met Grace and introduced her to the new facility. It was bigger than the office in Oregon, but it would also facilitate a child placement department. He realized that many children, like Michelle, may need to find a good, suitable home. He aimed to make this an addition to the existing foundations.

Grace interviewed until she had the right person for the job. It took several days, which placed her out of town on the expectant arrival of the family; however, she made haste and flew back Saturday morning with the first rays of the sun on

Sinclair's private plane.

Her return delightfully surprised her husband. He hadn't expected her back until the middle of next week, or he would have been at the airport when she landed. In fact, he was still in bed, sleeping soundly.

Ruth was the only one awake, besides Isaiah, who had gone to the barn. Delicious aromas wafted through the recently opened windows to the oncoming hostess. She could smell them as she walked up the drive. How she wished she could enjoy eating once again. Food still had that funny metallic taste. As it was, Grace simply continued to grow thinner each day. Her hair had begun to turn snow white, and consequently she decided to have it cut in Oklahoma. Since the red curls were fading fast, it looked odd to have white roots with red tails.

In the kitchen, she quietly welcomed Ruth, who stood astonished at the short hair. "Land sakes, Lamby! I doon't like it."

Grace just smiled brightly and crept soundlessly to her room and changed into a t-shirt and overalls. She smiled at the handsome sleeping husband. "God, what did I do to deserve such a wonderful man?" she thought. She put a straw hat over her crown to protect the already delicate skin from further damage, and then she was off to relieve Isaiah of his duties.

The day was beautiful. The mornings were still cool, and yet, the birds sang out in chorus, as if they were especially performing for them. Isaiah was working in his strawberry patch, as he normally did during this season. He received such a tranquility working in gardens. This contented him more than anything else he could have done. Grace noticed his handsome features across the field.

After giving him a welcome embrace, Grace began working on the fence they had begun before she left on her trip. They had already implanted the posts, which would surround the perimeter of selected pasture. Now, she began working on the cross posts. She worked silently, for the closest person was Isaiah, who was not even visible until she rounded the group of trees.

The sun was getting warmer, and Grace removed her straw hat and wiped the sweat from her brow. She had since rounded the corner and could see her sweet Scottish friend. Of course, Samson was right with her, waiting on her to give a command.

Travis and Brad were coming across the pasture to lend a hand, since Ruth told them Lamby had returned. Travis gave a loving rebuke to his wife for starting without waking him but took her order, as she put the two on separate posts. Travis received the one closest to the creek, while Brad began in the middle, working his way toward the creek. In the early afternoon, the two men met in the middle.

That portion was complete and she sent them to lunch with a promise that Grace would come when Isaiah did. Yet, when the two men returned from dinner, there was Grace and Isaiah, lost in their work. Grace was almost finished with the final section of the fence.

Travis began toward Grace with a reprimand. He intended to personally escort her to the house to eat. Then, he lost sight of her. She had vanished in thin air. They could still see Samson over the tall grass, which was ready to be cut for hay, but no Grace.

Grace To Cross The River

It is true that Grace had been diligent in her work, but something kept pulling at her to keep an eye on Isaiah. So as she worked, she also watched him work.

He rarely stopped. He worked on the runners, weeded, and fertilized. He fulfilled each task with utmost delicacy. He handled each tender leaf with care. Strawberries had been Isaiah's pride and joy for many years. They had enjoyed them with ice cream, shortcake, in preserves, and simply straight out of the patch.

This is how Grace came to witness his fall. A motion must have caught her attention out of the corner of her eye, for she did not see Travis and Brad coming back. Her head whirled toward the beloved to see what it was. Isaiah had, without a sound, placed his hand over his left breast. He staggered and fell to the ground.

Grace ran to his side calling, "Isaiah!" It took her a matter of seconds to reach him. She fell to her knees at his side, throwing her straw hat off.

"Hold on. I'll get some help. You'll be fine." She had taken his head in her lap and was coddling him with tears falling heavily.

His words were strained, but effective, "No, Grace. You and I both know it is time."

"I'd trade my life for yours, if I could." Two large tears splashed the man's rugged weather worn skin.

"No, Grace. It's my time."

"No, my beloved Isaiah. You cannot go. I need you. I love you. What will I do without you? You cannot leave me." His breath was hard, and he could not speak. Grace continued, "Had I helped more around here, you would be...I didn't do my share. I am so sorry. If you will stay here, I promise, you will not have to raise a finger for the rest of your life. I will do all the work."

He smiled weakly. "I doon't regret one minute. You have been a light for Ruth and me. We have enjoyed the years with you." He struggled to finish. "You have worked more than your share. One coold not have asked for a better daughter. It is not so bad, Grace." He closed his eyes and placed a contented smile on his lips. "I will see you on the oother side." His eyes opened again with alacrity. He tried to rise up, "The angels are here," he cried before slumping back.

Grace rocked his torso in her arms. She felt the last breath of life leave his body. The cold death crept over his body as she still held it close. "Noooo!" She cried aloud, as if begging God to wait a little longer to take her cherished from her.

Samson placed his soft muzzle next to Isaiah's cheek. He wanted to comfort his mistress in this time of grief. He gently snorted his bereavement.

It was Samson and her final cry, which led the two men to Grace's side. They entered into a realm that was not meant for them. They felt like intruders. Death announced itself clearly. Travis went to his wife's side, for lack of not knowing what else to do.

Isaiah's death devastated Grace. She could not help but to feel responsible for it. She knew he had been ill, yet she had not relieved his load any. Ruth, on the other hand, rose above the tragedy with grace. She was in love with her husband, but she loved him enough to let him go. She tried to be a comfort to Grace, but Grace grieved terribly.

Grace In Grieving

Although her health was improving, Grace never seemed to regain her former self. A sadness had dimmed the fire that once burned brightly through her violet eyes. Her heart tormented over the pain she blamed herself for causing her loved ones.

Her beloved Isaiah was buried on Sunday afternoon in a plot in her prayer garden. She decided to put a rock wall around the well-trodden ground in order to make in a small family cemetery. He loved the farm so well, that she knew he would want to be buried there.

Per Ruth's insistence Grace sang *his* song at his funeral. She lifted her sweet voice to Heaven and sang through the tears. *"Amazing grace, how sweet the sound, that saved a wretch like me."* She could hardly bring her voice to sound. *"I once was lost, but now, I am found, was blind, but now I see."* Everyone, save Ruth stood mesmerized. *"Twas grace that taught my heart to fear, and grace, my fears relieved. How precious did that grace appear, the hour I first believed."* She struggled to finish, and when she sang about the trials, her voice quivered and threatened to give out completely. Her Isaiah had seen many trials, and had come through each one with amazing grace.

"Through many dangers, toils, and snares, I have already come. Tis grace that brought me safe thus far, and grace will lead me home. When we've been there ten thousand years," Grace could not contain her emotions. Her hand erected in honor and praise to the Lamb that was slain. "Thank you, God for that amazing grace." She was saying to herself, while continuing. *"Bright shining as the sun, we've no less days to sing God's praise, than when we first begun."*

That was the only song sung at the informal burial, but every detail was just as Isaiah wanted it. Grace struggled to get through the song and remain standing. Weakness had overwhelmed her. His death was breaking her. Terry slipped her arm through Grace's, after she had finished.

"Lean on me cousin," she whispered.

Grace could not smile her thanks. She emphatically gave an expression of gratitude. She held to the cousin's arm and literally leaned on Terry. Then, God spoke to Grace in a still small voice. "This too, shall pass. Be still, and know that I *am* God. I am your Comfort in sorrow, and I will wrap My loving arms around you, for I have the whole world in the palm of My hand, and no thing shall come to pass without My consent."

Grace For Wendy

As Isaiah was laid to rest, a darkness fell, but God was bringing an answer to their prayers and closure to a trial.

The four young adults sat around a fire that night. Grace seemed distant during the somber converse between the others. She said nothing, yet she did not hear them. Renee had her investigator, who came to the funeral with her, at her apartment.

Travis played with the short strands of hair between his fingers that once held a rare color of fire. He had first seen the change when Grace threw her hat off to tend to Isaiah in the field, but that was an inappropriate time to mention it. As a matter of fact, now was an inappropriate time to tell her how much he disliked her hair short.

Incidentally, it was Wendy who broke the pall for Grace. For the weeks and months she had come to visit, she scrutinized her stepmother's every move and found nothing to be pretentious.

Several hours had passed since Amy and Michelle had fallen into the realm of dreamland, and they had hence heard Renee's company's car leave that Wendy came silently to the party. The evidence of tears still clung to her perfect complexion to tattle of how her hours had been spent. Grace shifted away from Travis for his daughter to have a place of comfort in her dad's arms.

But Wendy did not go to Travis. It was not her dad's comfort she needed. "I'm so sorry about Isaiah, Grace. I know you loved him very much." She spoke with a sweet consolation and wrapped her arms around her stepmother. She loved the old man, too.

Grace returned the embrace, stroking the shiny long hair. "Thank you." She held the girl in her arms, until Wendy pulled away.

She looked Grace in the eye. "I am sorry for the ugly way I have treated you."

Grace's charm returned in her smile, "I don't know what you are talking about." She immediately spoke her next sentence to prove to Wendy there was no need for absolution. "Someday, if you stay with us long enough, I'll tell you some wonderful stories about Isaiah. He was the closest person to perfect that ever lived, save Jesus Christ, who was perfect. Oh, and Wendy, he loved you so much. Just the other morning we went fishing, and his eyes would just twinkle when he mentioned your name." She winked, "I think he was partial to your brown eyes. He always had a soft spot for brown eyes."

117

Wendy smiled modestly, "Brown eyes are boring. It is like brown hair. It is common. Now, take your hair, for instance. Red is beautiful. Grace, why did you cut all the red off? You had such beautiful long hair."

"Oh, that. I guess I thought on the same lines as you. Red was boring, so I thought I should change for a while. But, I beg to differ with you." Grace smiled into her husband's eyes. "I think brown eyes are beautiful. I would never say boring."

"Well, I like your haircut," Terry interpolated. "It looks very stylish.

"I like it too," corrected Wendy, "but, I liked it better long."

They talked for hours more. Wendy felt more a part of a family than she had in many a year. Her stepmother proved to be most compassionate and understanding. Toward the early morning hours, a wonderful storm passed by, with winds blowing and trees raising their limbs to Heaven, while their leaves waved praise to the King of kings.

The morning broke sunny. Only those who had risen early enough to see the sun rise were witness to the incredible rainbow left in the wake of the tremendous rumblings of thunder. Grace smiled as she remembered the promise of that bow. God was indeed wonderful and worthy to be praised.

Wendy was the only other person in the household awake that early in the morning with the exception of Ruth. She met Grace in the barn and awaited for instructions from her new mom. "It is time I stopped being lazy and helped out around here," she explained at her appearance.

Grace Is No Surprise

Travis kept an eye on Singleton at the office. The man had turned cold and tried every day to fire Travis, hoping he would get tired of it and quit. Grace returned back to work with Renee as usual, but the security was set every time someone left or returned home. Wendy began getting involved with the foundation, trying to learn as much as she could about it. She would go daily with Grace, leaving Ruth, solely to give protection to Michelle during the day. Brad and Terry's week turned into two. They spent a couple nights on the coast, where Travis and Grace set up a cozy seaside cabin getaway for them.

Grace said nothing to anyone about the gnawing away inside her that someone was constantly watching her. On several occasions during the previous weeks, she had spotted a familiar black car in several of the places she happened to be. Travis mentioned nothing about similar experiences he was having. He did not want to worry Grace any more than necessary. Renee, Ruth, Amy, nor Wendy mentioned their suspicions either.

Because of the unanimous suspicions, everyone kept a special guard on the two young girls and protected them at every turn.

Brad and Terry decided it was Travis and Grace that should

get away for a weekend and made their plans with Travis to surprise Grace. As it stood, he and Grace had never been able to go on a wedding trip.

Friday evening, Travis would spring the plans on Grace, and the two of them would ride off into the sunset for a weekend of fun filled relaxation, or so he thought.

An important upcoming company meeting forced Grace to spend most of Thursday night trying to produce an accurate report from records less immaculate than her own. It is funny how two different people can keep such different habits. Grace was meticulous to account every penny with proof, and Renee was pretty good at keeping up with her. The other offices, however, were less than accountable for spending. It was easy to forget sometimes, to put an expenditure in the book when it was not immediately accessible.

Grace planted her work on the long Elizabethan chair in her study. She leaned back briefly to squeeze the jumble of numbers from the blackness of her closed eyelids.

Grace Through Adversity

She bolted awake at the loud ringing of the phone. The sun's rays were already peeping through the cracks of the shades. She had fallen asleep!

Grace ran to answer the phone, before it could ring twice and wake anyone else. "Hello," she heard Ruth answer and hung it back up. Seconds later, she heard Ruth, "Laddie."

Grace scrambled her many papers together and threw them on her desk, so that she would not be tempted to fall asleep again. Now, she must sort through these and find a reasonable amount to take to the office to work on.

"Honey," Travis came into the study, "have you been up all night?"

"No, I slept, trust me."

"Well, you didn't come to bed. You could not have slept much. We have a solution to that problem."

"We? Problem? Who are we, and what problem needs a solution?"

"Brad, Terry, Wendy, Ruth, and the girls, and oh yeah,

myself have made the arrangements for you to get away for a nice quiet weekend with the man who loves you most in the world."

"That sounds nice, but…"

The husband interrupted his rebuke, "Nope. There are no buts in this. You are going, and that my dear beautiful wife, is that."

She laughed as she answered the phone, which was ringing for the second time that morning. "Hello."

"Gracie. It is so good to hear your voice," a slimy horrid past came to life. "I need you to do me a favor. Dad's real sick. I have taken care of him for the last five years. I think you should volunteer to come be with him and take care of him for a while. So, here's what I am going to do. I am going to put him on the phone, and you behave yourself, and everything will be fine. If I hear one wrong word…well, I better not hear one wrong word, if you catch my drift. Here he is."

The once threatening boom had diminished into a pathetic meek voice. "Gracie, honey. We have looked for you for so long. I am so glad my prodigal daughter is coming home to take care of her daddy, while he is dying." His words rambled on meaningless.

Grace's mind was a whirlwind of thoughts and memories. How did they find her? She remained hidden for twenty plus years. How did this come to pass? She stood bewildered momentarily.

"I will kill you with my bare hands, before I ever let you get near my child," her brain screamed, yet she dared not say the words. Her brother's threat resounded. She knew he would follow through his threats.

The memories of what that voice brought to mind was tormenting to say the least. The recollection of his touch made her skin crawl.

A Debt Only Grace Can Pay

The floor fell from beneath her. Her heart beat erratically. She paled to a ghostly white. Her husband ran the length of the room to ensure her fall was in the chair behind the desk.

He snatched the phone, "Hello."

"Where is Grace?" replied a rough voice. "I want to talk to her."

"Who is this?" Travis's tone had changed to challenge the cruelty of the voice on the other end.

"Never mind. Let me talk to Grace."

"This is her husband. What can I help you with?"

"Just tell Grace to get to the phone." A few adjectives were thrown in for emphasis. "You're the husband? Well, this is her brother. Tell her if she don't get on the phone, I'm coming to her."

"What do you want with her?" Travis asked, remembering how much of an animal he was talking to. He knew very well what kind of person this was, and he was not about to let him bully his wife.

"She owes me and I'm ready to collect."

"She owes you nothing."

A cold sneering voice replied, "She owes me her life, or don't you remember? I saved hers."

"You were paid plenty for your service. If you think for one minute that you can get another dime out of Grace, you are most assuredly mistaken," Travis spat out angrily and would have hung up, had he not wanted to protect Grace.

"We'll see about that."

"Listen to me! You try to come anywhere near my wife, and I will have you arrested."

His threat was unheard. The call was stopped immediately by the loud bang of the receiver on the other end. Travis turned to his wife, who had recovered somewhat from the shock of hearing that voice after twenty-five years, but he met a fire like he had never seen before. He was not sure what the look meant, but he assumed he was getting ready to find out.

"What exactly did you pay that man for?" she minced no words.

A look of frightened confusion crossed. Ruth was just

returning from taking Amy to school, when she heard the commotion.

"What's all the shouting aboot?" She asked anxiously. "The wee oon will hear your loud voices."

Grace did not waiver from the sickening searching of her husband. Steady eyes showed him she wanted an answer NOW. Why did he feel like a naughty child getting caught with his hand in the cookie jar? He had done nothing wrong, but, he knew, by the vile in the brother's voice, he had done something terribly wrong. "Your bone marrow transplant. He was the donor. It was the only way to save your life. What else were we suppose to do?"

"Let me die." So much anger rose inside that she was barely able to speak. She trusted not her own reaction.

Ruth began a stream of mumblings heavy in the Scottish burr. Travis was now able to identify the fire. For the first time in his life, the man saw a real fear in his wife.

She continued through clenched teeth, "You take the one person in the entire world that could destroy everything we have and indebt me to him with my own life."

"But, you are not indebted to him. That is what you don't

127

understand. That man was paid good for his services."

"He was? Well I hope the price he demands is not more than you are willing to pay."

"Honey, he has already been paid," he argued.

"You are a fool if you think he has been paid." She never used the word 'fool'. It was wrong to call anyone a fool, but Grace needed to emphasize the importance of her words.

Travis took the rebuke to heart. He had never heard such cruel words uttered from her sweet lips. Still, he didn't fully understand. In a much more subdued and hurtful manner, Travis reiterated, "Then I was a fool. I was a fool in love and wanted to save your life more than better sense would allow me."

"And if I know my brother, the price was not cheap. Tell me, how much does selling your soul cost nowadays?"

Again, the words pierced the heart. "He was paid fifty thousand dollars."

"And might I ask where you got that kind of money?"

"Mr. Sinclair paid it." He was unable to look at her.

"Does everyone know, except me?"

Travis fought to defend their actions. "Grace, you were going to die. Neither of us wanted to do it that way. Had there been any other way in the world, we would have done it."

"I would rather be dead."

"That is selfish. We didn't want that. I do not know that I would do it differently, if given the opportunity to change it."

"Then you have sentenced me to worse than death. Do you seriously think he will stop at money?"

"He has to. You don't have to give him anything."

Grace prepared herself for the cup of bitter she was about to drink. She picked the phone up and dialed information to obtain his number.

"Why are you calling him back? I don't understand why you are calling him back."

"That's because you cannot fathom the Pandora's box you have opened." He still did not understand. "If I don't pay his price, his way, then he will take his pay any way he chooses. The man is a pedophile, do you dare consider what of mine he should choose?"

Grace In The Darkest Hour

She turned away to respond to the ringing on the line. "What do you want?"

The wicked response came, "I knew you're not stupid enough to not call back. You shouldn't have done that to Daddy."

"I will only ask one time more. What do you want?"

"Daddy wants to talk to you. First, I want you to listen to him. If you feel you can't be civil, remember this: you have two young daughters whom can make him happy if you can't."

Travis had never before heard the icy voice of his wife. "Put him on."

"Gracie, this is Daddy, honey. We've missed you around here. Your brother tells me he helped you out when you got sick. I'm glad to see you two have put your differences aside and become brother and sister again."

All Grace could do was let the tears quietly well up and overflow the ducts. Could she have been capable of hate, this would be the one she hated most. His words were lost, once again, to the angry thoughts consuming her attention. She held the phone in this manner for so long that Travis almost took possession of it again.

Finally, the weakened words tuned back into her listening capacity. "Can you do that Gracie? Daddy sure would appreciate it, honey. I know it must have been hard for you to need forgiveness all those years and never be able to get it. But don't you worry, Gracie, I will forgive you. We love you." The faux weeping commenced to sicken her bowels.

Shawn retrieved the phone. "That's a good girl, Grace. When are you coming?"

"What?" she asked in surprise.

"You told Daddy you'd come. When are you coming?"

She recalled his threat. "I don't know."

"That was for Daddy, now comes what I want. As you know, Daddy's dying. Since Mom died, he's had no one to care for him. I have taken care of him all this time, and I think the least you could do is cook and clean for him for his remaining time. He will not last much longer."

"I'll get back to you," was all she could think to answer.

He ended the conversation with a threat. "If I don't hear

from you within twenty-four hours, I *will* be knocking on your door."

Grace slammed the phone to its receiver, too angry to speak. With one last glimpse of her husband, she fled his presence.

Grace In Betrayal

She gave him a look of ultimate betrayal. He, whom had loved her most, hurt her the deepest. He had never seen her like this before. How was he to know? He would never intentionally have caused her one bit of pain. She must know that. If she had only told him. How could he be expected to help her, if she wouldn't meet him half way? Why couldn't she share some of the load with him? He loved her.

An engine revved as tires spun in the gravel. In an outrage, Grace left her briefcase and purse. The fiery rage inside heated her. Stupidly, she threw up to God, "What else can go wrong?"

The elderly, Scottish mother figure filled in the blanks. Both of her precious ones were in a state of devastation.

Travis had never known fear like this before. Something crawled inside him, leaving a demonic chill in its wake. Slowly, he was becoming painfully aware of what he had done. There was a sinking feeling in his heart that his actions would end up costing him more than he could bear.

"What have I done?" he asked Ruth.

"Don't worry Laddie, the good Shepherd watches for His lambs. Lamby, she ran froom the battle, a long time ago. He's just sending her back in to claim the victory. There will be Peace when the war is over."

"Everything sounds so simple, when you explain it, lovely Ruth. Too bad you can't explain it to my wife. I do not know if she will ever forgive me this time."

"There is no need for forgiveness, Laddie. Lamby's in shock. She's not been of right mind to take it to the Shepherd. Give her time. You moost troost her to do the right thing."

He treated her with a kiss. "You're right, as usual, lovely Ruth. Don't expect us tonight. I'm going through with my plans for the weekend. Alone time together is just what the doctor ordered."

She patted his cheek. "I'll be back. You go eat breakfast. You'll see, it will work oot according to His will. Lamby loovs ya mooch."

She had followed him to the kitchen with this last sentence and surpassed him into the living room and into their bedroom. After throwing a minimal of necessities together, she presented a duffel bag and suitcase.

134

The Plan Of Getting Grace

The man of the house left for work with a lighter heart. The day seemed to be the longest day ever. He tried to call his lover to make his apologies, but Renee said she was out. That was okay too. He would rather make them face to face, anyway.

There was not much to do at work, because Singleton had relieved him of most duties. The boss was trying to force Travis to quit. This had been escalating ever since the day Grace uncovered his discretions.

He completed the reservations for the weekend getaway, thinking how long he and Grace needed this time alone. They could talk about the demons, which forbade his lovely wife the peace and sanity she deserved. Obviously, she needed to be able to confide in him, something she apparently felt she couldn't do at this point. He loved her so. He did not ever want to put her in a position of being hurt again.

Brad and Terry were going to take the girls to the movies. Renee had plans with her new boyfriend, and Ruth planned on staying in, as usual. Travis would pick Grace up after he left work, and they would be off for the coast. That was the plan.

Slowly the clock ticked. Slowly the five o'clock hour drew

nigh. The lack of work gave him little to do, except tap his pencil on his desk and think about the events of the morning. What should he have done differently? Should he tell Mr. Sinclair that the brother was trying to get more out of his service? No, Mr. Sinclair had enough on his plate as it was. He would have to handle the brother himself.

He would simply have to explain to the scoundrel that he had his payment. Why should Grace fear this man? As the father, he would protect Amy and Michelle. That fiend would never get his hands on his girls. Furthermore, he would not get his hands on his wife. Grace was living in the past. She was a grown woman that should not fear the things that hurt her as a child. He didn't understand her strong protests.

Finally, the quitting hour came, and Travis wasted no time in leaving. He had seen Singleton leave about four o'clock, so he did not expect any delays in his plans. The boss wouldn't be there to give him any last minute tasks. He was free to go to his wife!

He talked to Renee a little earlier. She told him that Grace reported that she was going to work a little later tonight. He knew what that meant. Grace was going to avoid any confrontation tonight. She must not have had enough time to work through her anger yet. This would benefit his purpose. It

136

fit into his plans perfectly. He could pick her up at the office. He told Renee to explain to Ruth the new plan, and he would see her Sunday night.

The drive to his wife's office seemed to be the longest journey, with each mile bringing new anticipation at what her reaction was going to be.

There was no car in front of his wife's office. He would have to make sure to provide her with her transportation, again. Ever since he had moved to Oregon, she had given him full use of the Mustang, while she hitched rides with Renee, Stephanie, or even taxis. This was not proper for a lady of her stature.

He raced up the stairs two at a time. "Grace. Honey, where are you?" The office seemed empty. Again, he called out, "Grace. I am sorry for this morning. Honey, I have a surprise for you. Grace? Are you here?" He walked to her closed office door. It was locked. "Well she must have already left," he thought to himself.

Another Graceful Disappearance

Next, he left for the house. Maybe she had forgiven him after all. He hadn't gotten very far down the road, when the phone in the Mustang rang clear. He conjured a happy tone. "Hello."

"Ooh Laddie. I'm so wooried. I don't oonderstand what's hap'nin," Ruth spat out in much too excited tongue, that Travis almost didn't understand her.

"Whoa. Ruth. What do you mean? What happened?"

"It's Lamby. She called the house and told me to code green, boot I'm here all by me self. I don't know where the lassies are."

"Did Grace say where she was?"

"No, no. She didn't sound like herself. Soomthin's wrong. I can feel it in me bones."

"What exactly did she say?" Travis asked intently.

"She said, 'Are the chilr'n home?' I said, 'no.' She said, 'Code green.' After that, she hoong oop and never called back."

"I don't know what to tell you. If Terry and Brad get back with the girls, secure them. I will get back in touch with you as soon as I can. There is an officer behind me with his blue light on. I have to pull over. I will call you back when I can."

He slowed the car to a halt and rolled down his window. He could see the officer in the mirror approaching his vehicle, studying it carefully.

The officer asked him politely, "You are Grace's Sorenson's husband, aren't you?"

"Yes sir."

"You didn't happen to pick her up at her office, did you?"

"No sir. I went by, but she wasn't there. What's going on?"

"We'd like for you to come back with us."

Travis questioned again, "Why? What is going on? What's happened to my wife?"

"That is what we would like to know."

Grace Vanishes

As he spoke, a third car, which had pulled up during the initial questioning, opened its doors and let out two men clad in dark suits. Travis was not sure whether they were accusing him of something or not.

One man approached as if he had the right to intrude. "Does he have her?"

The officer answered, "No."

"Dang it. How did we let this happen? Hurry up. Let's get back to the office. She couldn't have disappeared without a trace." He turned to the other man in the suit. "Cole, drive his car. He'll ride with me." He whisked Travis by his arm toward his car.

Travis could see the Mustang and the police car following behind. The driver's voice was deep. "What do you know about your wife? Would she disappear without letting anyone know?"

Travis was fed up with the secrecy he was being held in. "I am not saying one word about my wife until you tell me what is going on. Why do you want Grace, and who are you anyway?"

At first, he thought the man would refuse to answer. Then slowly, "I'm Leo. We are FBI. We have been watching your family. Graham Sinclair called us right after you spoke with him. Thanks to your wife, we are investigating Ron Singleton in connection with some abductions in this area. We were alerted on this matter, but could manage to get no leads on it. Once your wife pointed the finger at the culprits to Graham Sinclair for child abusers, we began connecting the dots." They parked the car in front of Grace's office. He continued. "We have had men on every member of your family. Tonight, though, we seem to have lost your wife. Somehow, she slipped through our fingers."

Travis was at loss for words. He hadn't realized they were watching every move his family made. As the four men loaded the elevator at Grace's office, Leo continued his explanation. "My partner and I followed your sister's car at approximately four fifty-two with two people in it." He stopped talking long enough for him, his partner, and the officer to draw their guns.

They stepped off the elevator in a professional manner, checking all corners and doors. The partner came out of Grace's office. "No one in there. She's not here."

Travis stepped in, "I don't understand. If two people were in Renee's car, you have your answer. Grace has been riding with her, since she was run off the road."

"No, Mr. Winston. She was not the second person in the vehicle. "

Travis thought back to his first visit. "Wait a minute. When I came by earlier, her office door was locked. How is it open now?"

"Very good question. Colin, search the office." The partner and officer disappeared into the room. Leo went on to explain to Travis. "Are you familiar with a man by the name of Steve Jenson?"

"Steve, yeah. He is dating my sister."

Leo shook his head sadly. "That was his cover. He tried to take Miss Winston by force tonight. Fortunately, we were trailing her and happened to see it. We aren't sure what his connection is, if any, to the abductions, but your sister is at the hospital getting checked out."

"Why the hospital?" he demanded.

"Like I said, sir, he tried to take her by force. Your sister is a spunky little one."

Travis's fists clenched tight. "Where is he? I'll ..."

"Leo," interrupted Colin. "I think you should hear this." He led them over to Grace's desk. Inside the open drawer, Travis could see her tape recorder. Colin finished. "We were checking out things in here, when we heard a click from this drawer. We believe it was this tape player. We didn't hear any music, so we assume she was recording something."

"What is this?" Leo asked, picking up the phone receiver. "This is blood."

Travis grew scared. "Oh Father. Please let her be safe. Help me to find her in time. In Thy holy name, I pray," he uttered.

Leo asked, "Where'd it come from? Any more?"

They searched carefully, but could find only some in one spot on the floor near the door. The officer propped against the door, waiting for the two comrades to inspect the spot on the floor. His hand slipped. Looking down, he saw more of the red fluid.

"Here is more. I'm sorry I messed up the print. I didn't know it was there."

"It looks like she grabbed on. Since there is so little blood, it does not look as if she was hurt very bad. Possibly, she injured her hand. Colin, see if you can find anymore blood in the building."

"Let's listen to the tape."

They waited impatiently for the machine to rewind, but before it finished, Colin and the officer came back and explained their findings.

"We found some on the outer door, so we came back up the stairs, and there was some on the railing and door leading to the stairs. It still has a red color. It looks fresh. She could not have been here more than ten, fifteen minutes, tops. Probably less."

"Did you look around outside?" Leo asked.

"Yep. Not a soul in sight."

"Maybe this tape will tell us something."

Preparations Of Grace

When Grace left home that morning, she was blinded by rage. Oh, how her heart broke from the betrayal. How was she to deal with the devil? She cast these people aside years ago, hoping never to be reminded of their existence. Would she ever be free of them again?

She knew what she must do. There was no choice. It may destroy her marriage and family, yet that was better than destroying her child. She could never explain where she was going, or what she was doing. They must never find out.

Work was the last thing on her mind. She came to the realization that she could not leave her girls without saying a word to them, so she picked Amy up during her lunchtime to explain what little she could.

They sat over their food at the restaurant, after having asked the blessing. "Amy, I know I have been a lousy mother. I have not been around enough."

"Oh, but you're wrong. You are the perfect Momma. I know you have to go on business a lot."

For a eight-year-old, she seemed very grown up. Grace

smiled, "You are such a big girl. Sometimes, we must do things we do not like doing. I love you and Michelle very much."

"Do you have to, Momma?" the golden child asked. Grace shifted in her chair. Amy knew the answer and spoke sadly. "We understand. Will you be gone long?"

"I must go away for a long time, this time. I cannot get out of doing this task before me. I hope your dad will understand as well as my golden girl. I promise, after I get back this time, I'll not leave you again, if I can help it. I plan on retiring from work and dedicating all my time to raising you and Michelle. God did not give me two beautiful girls to raise for nothing. I want to teach you both to ride and show horses. It is a good outlet for you both. There is a young man, who lives down the road from us that can begin the lessons, while I am gone. Will you both do that for me?"

"When are we going to adopt Michelle? I can't wait for her to be my real sister. I always wanted a sister, and a brother. Maybe we can adopt a brother, too."

Grace smiled, "We'll see. It is not ours to know what God has in store for us."

"I will pray every day that God will return you home soon," Amy announced.

146

"Oh, I need that more than you will ever know. Pray that I will always do His will too. He knows best."

Graceful Goodbye

Having told Amy, Grace felt able to make the phone call in
which she so dreaded. She couldn't make it just yet. She would
take advantage of the full twenty-four hours given to her. She'd
go to the office and prepare Renee to take over the reins
permanently. She would contact Mr. Jameston in New York to
turn in her notice. She detested the idea of leaving him in the
lurch like this, but it was necessary.

She waited to ascend the old familiar stairs, looking, for the
last time, at the beauty this old place held. This building may be
just an old eyesore for many, but she knew how it was from the
inside. The large pillars supported her weight for nigh on
fifteen years. Their shadows had welcomed her many mornings,
as they had waved her goodbye many evenings.

She touched one pillar, then another, as if it were an old
friend. Most people would be scared to come into this place
alone, but not her. When she first came to work in Springfield,
she had cast her a cot, right back there in the shadow behind the
last pillar on the right. She lived here, until she was able to find
the farm. God had taken care of her even then. He would
surely see her through this trial.

She breathed in the old air in the stairway. The door echoed as it shut. Each step resounded. This would possibly be the very last time she climbed these stairs. Well, plans must be made.

"Renee, are you working on the Hollis case?"

"No. I interviewed Glenda, but I needed you to follow up. I think it would be to her benefit to talk to you," said the sister-in-law.

"You must trust your judgment, dear sister. You are no fool. The girl could only be helped from you being in charge. What other open cases do we have?"

Renee counted her fingers. "Bradley, Gazzly, Hollis, Peterson, and Stepp. I think that's all of them. Gazzly goes to court in three weeks, Peterson next month, and of course, Michelle day after tomorrow."

"Yes, I'll be so glad when that one is finally over. Travis and I plan on starting the adoption proceedings, when it all gets settled."

Renee clapped excitedly, "I am so glad. I figured you would. Hey, would you care if I took off a little early today? Steve said he had a surprise for me and wanted me to get off as early as I can."

"Sure. Just leave whenever. I will probably work a little late tonight, so if you happen to see your brother, will you let him know for me?"

"Sure thing. He called a little while ago for you."

"Okay. I will be in my office, so whenever you need to take off is fine with me."

Grace sat down at her desk. Renee came in momentarily, bringing in all the current files for her boss. She patted Grace's head on her way out to show her sisterly affection.

Grace stared unseeingly at the task before her. Where to begin? Well, Renee rattled them off alphabetically; maybe she should do them in that order. Carefully, she wrote specific notes on each of the folders, except for Michelle's. That one would take special handling. She specified what each one needed in order to be completely successful. Of course, she used her trusty tape recorder to leave audible instructions to boot. The pause button was certainly being used today.

She ran out a little before four o'clock to run to the bank and to obtain some information at the courthouse. Also, she wanted to explain to Stephanie her intentions.

Renee popped in a little later to say goodbye. "Are you sure you are okay to stay here by yourself? I mean, after everything that has happened."

Grace laughed, "I am fine. You go on out with your private investigator and have fun."

"Oh, I almost forgot. My brother called, while you were out. I gave him your message," Renee spoke as she made her way to leave.

"Thank you. I'll see you later, my dear."

Grace could hear a faint, "goodbye" coming as the elevator bell dinged.

She began her duties once again. "Regarding Michelle Bradley," she spoke to the recorder. "I have locked in a safe deposit box at Springfield National Bank, the pertinent information which will exonerate Michelle from man one. Stephanie has the necessary identification to open it."

She heard a noise in the outer office. "Did you forget something, Renee?" She didn't even look up from her writing. "Did you say you told Travis I'd be late?"

"I sure hope so." The door closed. "You're going to be."

Grace And The Devil

Grace jerked her head up at the masculine voice. "What do you want?" she asked in annoyance. This was all she needed today.

"Did you think I would forget my promise to you? I told you to stay out of my way, but you wouldn't listen. I received my subpoena. I warned you, Mrs. Winston, now it is time to pay the piper."

"I don't care about your threats. You do not scare me." She stood to quickly shuffle the papers before her, so that he would not see Michelle's file. "You failed at your first attempt, and I assure...ouch! What was that?"

Ron Singleton coyly locked the office door behind him and drew close to her, while she was preoccupied with the file. Now, he stood grinning an evil that made her shudder, while holding an empty syringe. "Oh, this little thing. It is called heroine. Have you ever taken it before, Mrs. Winston? If you are a virgin to the substance... I sure hope I didn't give you too much. From my understanding, too much can lead to quite a painful death."

Grace couldn't control the rage inside, which made her

blood boil faster, in return, pumping the evil through her veins faster. Her head had already begun to get dizzy. She squinted to make a clear vision. "Your threats don't frighten me."

"Oh, but my dear, you better be very frightened. Welcome to hell."

"What makes you think I would do anything you say?"

"Because, I have what you love most. Do you recognize the man in this picture?"

Grace tried to focus on the picture of Steve and Renee. Renee was bound. "What about him?"

"Why, he is one of us. Your sister-in-law was an easy snare. You'll do what I say, because you don't want that young woman spoiled."

Grace thought of lunging toward him, and physically defending Renee, but her brain wouldn't function in the capacity necessary for doing so.

He continued, "Furthermore, we hold those two precious little girls of yours. They did not quite enjoy that movie. Oh, I see you don't believe me. Well, pick up the phone and call home. Ask that housekeeper where they are. I assure you that they are not where they are suppose to be."

Grace's movements were already being hindered. She fumbled with the phone. There was difficulty in dialing. At last she heard Ruth's voice. "Ruth, are the children home?" she asked anxiously.

Ruth responded in her usual sweet voice, "No."

"Code green!" Grace spat out quickly. Suddenly there came a sharp pain in her right hand, as Singleton had pierced it with a blade.

"What was all that 'code green' stuff about?" He became angry at her refusal to answer. "No matter. It won't help you now. So, tell me. Was I right? Are the kids where they are safe?" He had his arm around her, holding the point of the knife to her throat.

Grace was getting weaker. She blinked several times to clarify her vision. But, she refused to answer. Her world was quickly becoming a hallucination.

Singleton pressed the wound in her hand and pressed the point of the knife into her tender flesh. "Now, here are the rules. Rule one, when I ask a question, you answer it. Rule two, I am in control. Rule three, when I tell you to beg, you beg. It's that simple. Do you understand?"

She nodded in affirmation.

"We have such wonderful plans for you and those brats, and for Miss Winston. Would you care to hear them?"

"You'll not touch them." She struggled to remain lucid.

In his anger at her defiance, he pressed the knife, until a little blood oozed out. "Rule two: I am in control. What do you think you can do about it?"

Her fingers were dancing with long bending curves. She was finding it harder to concentrate. "You can do what you want with me, but you leave those children and Renee alone."

"And that leads to rule number three. If I remember correctly, I told you that day in my office that you would beg me to hurt *you*. And looky here what we have. Okay, I am ready. Beg."

He was forcing her to her knees by crushing her injured hand. Tears were coming, but not because of being hurt. She had begun to fear for her children. She would beg, borrow, or steal to protect her children. She was not too proud, and she was used to pain. She would do anything he asked, as long as he left the innocent alone.

"I am begging you. Please, let them go. You can do what you want to me, just let them go."

"Is that the best you can do?" He drew closer to her face. "Michelle begged better than that."

Grace lunged forward to strike, but her slow reactions allowed him to dodge the swing. In her mind, she could see Michelle being ripped from her car and dragged in the woods. She was dead or unconscious. Grace could not tell, but the person was no longer Michelle, it was Renee. Steve had a shovel over one shoulder, and was dragging Renee by her feet. "Please, let her go!" she cried loudly. "Somebody help her!"

His hand cupped her mouth tightly, hindering her from breathing. She struggled for each breath. "Shut up! Don't you scream, again. Now, I am going to take my hand from your mouth, and if I hear one more scream, you will never see Renee again and those two girls will rue the day you entered their lives. That is why you will be a good girl and keep it shut, isn't it?" He tightened his grip. "I said, isn't it?"

She affirmed with a nod of the head. He did not yet remove his hand. "Shall I tell you what is going to happen to you? We have a load to take to South America tonight. That little sample of goodies I gave you is the first of many. By the time you reach your destination, you will do anything for your next fix. They love to enslave beautiful women, but in your case, you may be too old, and your beauty has faded. They would love to make sport of you though. How does that sound to you? You're a feisty one. They would enjoy watching you, I am afraid. Don't you think you'd enjoy that?" She nodded, "Now, how badly do you want to spare them?" This time, he removed his hand slowly.

"Please," she almost whispered through tears. "I will do whatever you say. Please, leave them alone. I am yours to do what you will."

"You can't beg very well, but that is a start. I suppose I can't sell the product without testing the goods. What do you say?"

Her brain was playing tricks on her. He kept wavering in between the vision of her father, her brother, Travis, and himself. She could not be sure of who was really before her. She was unable to stand on her own, since he had deprived her of enough air.

Singleton hesitated his actions, when he heard Travis calling for Grace. "Ah looky, here. Dear old husband to the rescue.

Don't make a sound. I would hate to have to take those two pretty little girls along with you tonight. If he comes in, you get to watch him die." He was whispering close to her ear. He stopped, when Travis tried the knob.

Intoxicated Grace

Grace closed her eyes tightly to squeeze out the unreal. Her salvation had come. She managed a hoarse, futile whisper, "Help," but she dared not breathe too loudly for fear he might actually hear.

Upon hearing the retreat, Singleton began again, "That's a good girl. See, I don't even have to use my knife with you. Dear hubby doesn't know you just saved his life. I never figured you for being such an easy puppet. I say, though, you don't deserve that husband you got. He's not much for supporting you, is he? Any man that would let the woman do all the fighting ain't much of a man, I'd say. But, that will fit in well, where you're going."

Grace was losing the battle for control of her mind. She could hear Travis's voice, but to her, it was a voice from the past that sent a fear through her strange body. "Please daddy, it hurts. I'll be a good girl. I won't ever tell anybody, I promise."

Singleton laughed and made sport of her hallucinations, "You won't tell? Well Grace, how did everyone find out? You know you must be punished."

"I won't tell daddy's secret. I promise. Stop Shawn. It

hurts."

Ron Singleton would have continued his torture, but a thought had come to him that Travis may come back. It was time to get her to the plane, gather the two brats, and Renee, and get them out of the country, before trouble came.

"Come on princess, time to go. Remember, one false move, and your sister-in-law and daughters will take this trip with us."

He dragged her half walking, because she had no control of her legs. They descended the stairs, and were barely in the shadows of the first floor, when he heard someone coming in the front door. He pulled her behind a pillar and waited for them to be enclosed in the elevator, and then, he made his escape. Around the corner, he forced the helpless woman into his car.

He raced to the point of rendezvous. "Where are Jensen and Meyers? Where're the kids and girl? Are you all helpless?"

The other man responded, "I haven't seen them yet. Calm down, Singleton, they'll be here. We have a foolproof plan. You worry too much."

"I know Jensen has been tested and proven, but are you sure we can trust Meyers? Somebody better worry. You'll go down with the rest of us if something goes wrong. I had the hardest one, and I'm already here. They should have beaten me here."

"They'll be here. Come on. We can get everything ready to fly as soon as they get here. Toss her in the baggage hole. She can't do any damage down there."

Singleton obeyed the order. He threw her into one of the many large cages in the cargo hold and locked the door securely behind him. He secured the outside door, and then came back in the terminal. He began again, "I will wait until seven o'clock. If they're not here, we are leaving without them. I am not going to risk getting caught. We have got to get this one out of the country before anything goes wrong. I am telling you now, we should have heard something by now."

It was quarter till seven. Singleton was getting very antsy. "I say we get outta here. Meyers and Jensen should've been here by now. Something's gone wrong. It'll be bad enough, if they get caught, but we're not going to get caught? This cargo will end us in jail for the rest of our lives. Are you willing to take that risk?"

"Tell the pilot to fire up. I'll shut the door," his partner ordered. "Maybe we need to stay out of the country until we find out if they have been caught."

Singleton entered the cockpit. "We're taking off. Let's go."

The two men settled into their seats, snapping their seatbelts around them. "Ah, another load, free and safe," bragged the judge.

Ron looked nervously out of the window. "I'll feel better once we're in the air."

Hearing No Grace

Travis listened to the words that Ron Singleton spoke on the recorder. His vengeful anger turned to guilt as he listened. He could hear his own voice faintly in the background. He had been outside the door when this monster was…Grace…He could have stopped him. He could have saved Grace. Why didn't he think it odd that the door was locked? Why did she not call out to him? He knew why. He heard the awful threat. She would have suffered any torment to save Amy and Michelle from harm. Where did that leave him? It is easy to condemn and judge when you're not the one being threatened.

His heart broke when he heard his wife's pitiful plea for help from her own father, and then her brother. He was just beginning to see a little of what Grace had suffered through. Now, this fiend knew it as well and was exploiting her insecurities. Now, her devoted husband had put her life in even more danger than he ever dreamed. He should have considered the outcome of using Shawn's marrow. Ron hit the nail on the head when he said Travis was not a man.

His admiration for his wife grew. She was, indeed, a creature of rare character. Not many other people held the qualities that Grace did. Even with an evil substance coursing through her veins, she fought hard and achieved more than he had been straight. He, and those precious children, had been her sole focus. She had cared nothing for her own safety. Could he have been half of what she was, she would have reason to be proud of him. No, she had no reason to be proud of him.

Leo was on the phone in private converse. His radio had gone off, and he excused himself to use the phone. The officer and Colin were still searching for clues.

"Shep," Leo hung up the phone. "Take Mr. Winston home."

Travis protested, "No way. That is my wife out there."

"I think it would be better if you left this part for us. You are needed at home," Leo insisted.

"Better for whom? If you don't find my wife, it is only a statistic. If I don't find my wife, it is my life. If you think I am going to sit at home, while my wife is in danger, you are mistaken."

Grace For Children

The FBI agent sounded less pleasant, "That call was from the agents following your daughter and Michelle Bradley. There has been an attempt on their lives."

"Are they safe?"

"They were abducted from the theatre. Our men were following and able to prevent it from happening."

"Are they safe?"

"They are. They are taking them home."

Travis concluded with finality, "Then my place is with my wife."

"Colin, you and Shep go together, and Winston will ride with me." He spoke, as they left the building.

Travis could not forget the words of his boss. They resounded in his brain. "You will do anything for your next fix…enslave beautiful women…make sport of you…you are a feisty one." He dreaded the thought of the answer to the question burning in his mind.

"Sir, Singleton said something about getting a load up tonight. What was he talking about?"

"I am afraid, I don't know." He had his own idea, but the answer frightened him. There was no sense upsetting this woman's husband for nothing. Besides, if they did not make it in time, her loved ones would never see her again.

Travis knew the only solution. He bowed his head and prayed aloud, "Please, God keep her safe, and please help us to get there in time."

"So, you are a praying man, huh? I hope He answers."

Travis shook his head. "He will." Travis felt like a suck egg dog. The Word said that Christ would be a father, brother, or friend. He had always been there for Grace, unlike himself, who had let Grace down over and over.

The airport was not near the office. It was nearer to Eugene, where planes were in the process of landing and taking off. Leo had no idea which plane belonged to Sinclair Airlines, but Travis could recognize it.

The agent flashed his badge, which allowed them all entrance to the plane section. They were almost to the point of assuming the plane was gone, when a familiar wing came in sight. It taxied out of the hangar at the end of the runway.

"There it is!" Travis shouted.

Leo's hand went quickly to his hip. He spoke into his radio, "The small plane on the runway. Stop it!"

But, the plane taxied on.

Wings Of Grace

"That plane better not leave the ground," he threatened into the radio.

"Flight 33SA24, please return to the hangar." The tower was commanding on the plane's radio. "I repeat, 33SA24, abort. You will be stopped by force, if you do not pull over. All other flights, please abstain from lift off. Flights will be delayed. I repeat; all flights please abstain from liftoff. All flights out are delayed."

"It looks like it is slowing," Travis shouted.

"Come on." Leo led the group, while security vehicles were pulling quickly onto the runway.

One vehicle stopped beside them. "Hop in," the driver shouted.

Leo and Travis were the only ones that mounted the vehicle. It was a matter of seconds, before they were beside the aircraft. A man had already been escorted from the plane. He was cooperating as far as Travis could see.

168

Within a moment, Singleton was descending the steps in protests. "I am the president of Sinclair Airlines. You have no right to confiscate this plane. It is all legitimate. I have all my paperwork in order."

Leo stepped into the conversation, "What is the purpose of this flight, Mr. Singleton?"

"Judge Harris hired us for a private plane."

"And you are using a cargo plane as a private plane?" asked Leo.

"Unfortunately, it was the only one available. We have done business with the judge before. We value his business and would like to keep on his good side. That's why I am appalled at having been stopped as if I am a common criminal. What is all this about?"

Leo touched his arm. "Will you come with us, please?" He directed him to a security officer. "Take him to a separate room than the judge please. I will be there in a few minutes."

Immediately, Leo burst through the plane's doorway. Travis followed suit. There was not much to search through. The confused captain allowed them access to every spot in the plane.

Travis's heart was failing. There was no sign of his beloved. If they could not find the proof on the plane, they may never find what he did with Grace.

Found Grace

"Well, Mr. Winston. It looks as if we may have made a bad call. There is only one more place to look, but I doubt she will be there." He led the expectant husband to the outside of the plane. "Open this," he ordered the airport worker, which stood nearby.

The young man in uniform lifted the lock and then the latch to the cargo hold. They all stood back for a brief period, astonished at the sight before them.

Four large cages stood before them, looming in the shadows, where the sun could not reach. Inside the cages were young boys and girls. Some sat shielding their eyes from the over abundance of light now filtering through the darkness they had become accustomed to. Some were lying in slumberous piles. There was Grace, laying in a heap, oblivious to the world.

"Oh my…" The worker stood dumbfounded. Realizing that he may be blamed, he quickly added. "We did not load this plane. We had no knowledge of this."

"Get these cages unlocked," ordered Leo. Then, turning to Travis, "That is your wife, isn't it?"

"Yes," He answered and ran to it.

"Stand back," Leo ordered, as he took out his gun and shot the lock. It fell to the ground noisily.

Travis ran in. The noise of the gun startled Grace awake, but when Travis started toward her, she recoiled. She held her hands out to keep him in abeyance. Her glassy eyes focused on something unreal, where her brain had been poisoned.

Her words were mumbled, "Nnoo. Please daddy, don't let him. It hurts too bad, now."

Travis stopped in his tracks. She was genuinely petrified. He could hear something frantic in her voice. He did not want to frighten her, but he couldn't leave her in despair of her fears. After a hesitation, he proceeded. He rushed to her side and seized her in his strong arms against her protests.

He gently laid her on a cot, which the ambulance had brought upon arrival. More sirens and lights were coming across the runway, where Leo had called the tower. Travis didn't stick around to find out what was going to happen to any of the children or Singleton or Harris. He loaded in the ambulance with Grace. He was unable to get next to her, because the paramedic was working continually over her fighting body. She was still confused and disoriented.

No Knight For Grace

Travis called home from the hospital, where Brad and Terry confirmed they had already secured the code green. They assured Travis, that the girls were doing well. None had any knowledge of what was going on with Grace. He could not endure telling them what Grace had been through. That would come soon enough. Least of all, he didn't want the children to know.

"How is she?" Renee asked as soon as they saw Travis.

He was sitting in a chair outside her door, his hands cupping his rugged face. The emotional stress of the day had worn him. Upon hearing Renee, he looked up.

"She is still sleeping."

"What happened, Laddie?" Wendy supported Ruth down the hall.

"Wendy, what are you doing here? I thought you were staying with Amy and Michelle."

"No dad, my place is here with you and Grace. Terry and Brad are with them."

173

He couldn't think straight enough to smile, but he was grateful that his daughter had come around. He dropped his head into his hands again. Tears found their way down his cheeks. "It is that blamed job of hers. She deals with the lowest criminals on the earth. She went too far this time, and they almost got Renee and the girls right along with Grace."

"Travis, I am sorry I didn't use better judgment with Steve. I should have known he was a jerk. We know what happened with the girls, but what happened with Grace?" Renee asked.

"He got her after you left. He shot her up with heroine so she could not defend herself."

"Ooh my dear Lord!" exclaimed Ruth.

"Thank the Lord we found her in time." He chose not to reveal any more than that for now. He couldn't bear to utter the words of all that had happened, let alone to think of what they were going to do with all those children. He looked angrily toward Ruth. "She should have told me. You should have told me. I might have been able to protect her, had I known."

He was guilty of not protecting her, and that weighed heavily on his conscious. He didn't mean the harsh angry words, but it seemed easier to share the blame with someone else, even if it was Grace.

174

Renee frowned at the mystery between her brother and Grace, but Ruth understood. "Ooh Laddie. She has her reasons. You cannot blame her. She moost deal with her demons in her own way, joost like you and me."

"Dad. I can't believe you," Wendy rebuked.

He wiped a tear from his face. "She is right. Ruth, I apologize. I am just so angry at myself. I don't mean to take it out on you, or Grace." His shoulders began to shake from crying. "I prayed to God that if He let her be safe in Ireland, I would love her and take care of her for the rest of her life, and I have failed miserably. She has been anything but safe."

"Laddie…"

Ruth was stopped short by a sudden shout from within the room. "Nooooo." Grace called and bolted upright.

Coming To Terms Of Grace

Ruth ran in, but Travis remained. "Lamby!" She ran to the side of the bed. Grace was hyperventilating. Her head was wet from the heat of her body. Her eyes were wild, as she doubled over in pain. Ruth laid her back and caressed her brow. "Ruth's here, now, Lamby. It's all gonna be alright now." She pulled the shaking form into her bosom. "Shh, shh, now. Ruth's here."

"Oh! Ruth, it hurts so much. What happened? Why does it hurt?" She pulled away from the security of Ruth's arms, grabbed the rail of her bed, and frantically tried to pull out of the bed.

Ruth assisted her out of the bed, and Grace ran to the bathroom. Again, Ruth was by her side, gently stroking her hair. "Doo ya not remember? Come on. Let's get you back in bed. You need to rest."

Wendy had come in to see what was going on with Grace and helped Ruth get her back into the bed. She said softly. "Grace, are you okay?"

Grace searched her with her eyes unknowingly. She did not know the girl. "What are you doing here?"

"You are my new mother. Where else would I be? I love you and don't want you to go through this without knowing that."

Grace tried to remember the face, but could not. She double over in pain. "Oh!"

Ruth calmed her again, wiping her sweaty brow. "Shh. Lie back, Lamby. Get soom rest."

Grace fell back helplessly and closed her eyes. Before long, she was dreaming the horrors, which tormented her, again. She lay like this for around ten minutes, before she shot up again, screaming, "Nooo!"

This continued all night. What horrors she suffered while on the heroine, only God knew. Prior to Ruth's coming, Travis had tried to approach his wife several times. He wanted to comfort her, but she would shrink back in a frightened withdrawal. At last, he stopped trying. It broke his heart. He could not understand that the evil in her veins deprived her of any sense of reality. She recoiled at the nightmare in which she was living, not at the real man before her.

Renee stayed all night with her brother. Wendy came out several times during the night to fetch coffee or something to eat for Ruth, Renee, and Travis. It was a long night for the husband to suffer.

When morning broke, and he still had not been in to see Grace, Renee became annoyed. "What is going on? Why aren't you in there with her? She is going through something awful."

The man remained with his head in hands. "She does not want me in there. She is afraid of me. Can you believe it? My own wife cannot stand the sight of me. I don't blame her. I would hate me too, if I stood by while some lowlife..." His voice trailed off.

"What happened, Travis?"

"Another day, sister, another day."

The doctor who admitted Grace came into the room with her chart in hand. "Who are you?" he asked, while looking at Ruth and Wendy.

Wendy explained their relationship and the fact that her dad was right outside the door. The doctor asked Wendy to leave. He thought she was too young to be in the room, while he talked to Grace. When Wendy had no choice but to comply, Renee took her to the cafeteria to gracefully allow them the privacy needed.

When Grace Fails

"Mrs. Winston, how are you feeling?"

She had started acknowledging reality a little more. Grace thought, "Why is it that doctor's always ask that question? How do they think you are feeling, when you are in the hospital?" In response to his question, "I have been better."

"The neurologist worked on reconnecting the nerves which were severed in your hand. It should not give you any trouble. However, if you notice any bleeding, numbness, or impotency, see your regular doctor. How are you otherwise? Do you still feel disoriented?"

"Everything is confusing and blurry. My whole body burns."

"That is natural. Heroine can do a lot more than that, but I have another concern with the effects of the drug." He flipped the papers on her clipboard. "Lab brought me the results from the rape kit. I must ask you, Mrs. Winston, were you pregnant?"

"No. Why?"

"There is no easy way of telling you this. The test from the rape kit tested positive for pregnancy. Women who use drugs during pregnancy increase the chances of birth defects. We will want to run more tests later on. Other than that, you are well enough to go home. I will send the nurse in with the paper work and instructions. You need to see your gynecologist as soon as possible."

Inside the room, Grace struggled to keep the tears from embarrassing her. Outside her door, her husband felt the last straw break her spirit. He had done this. In allowing that man to get his wife, he allowed this to happen to Grace. She should hate him for the rest of her life. Grace's next words sealed the decision of her husband to exile himself from her. He didn't blame her.

"Lamby," Ruth was saying, "Should I call Laddie in?"

"No," Grace said sharply. "I can't face him right now." Indeed, the wounds from the morning were still fresh. She was not ready to smile and say, 'everything is great'. He had done the unforgivable, and now, she must do the impossible. Just because this had happened, the problem of yesterday still needed a solution. To top it all off, she had just been told that she had been impregnated by a rapist. How could he ever stand the sight of her again?

180

"Ooh, boot Lamby, he loovs you."

"And how much do you think he will love me when he finds out about this? Do you think he will want to love me while I am carrying some other man's child? Do you honestly think he will want to raise a monster's child, look at him for his entire life, while trying to love him as his own?"

"Joost tell him the whole truth."

"I can't."

Ruth pressed her hand on Grace's. "How doo ya expect to live with a man, if ya cannot tell him the truth? He deserves to know, after all this time."

"How should I tell the man I love more than my own life these things too unbearable to speak? My heart hides them deep, so that I may not bear this horror. How should I begin, dear Ruth?" She spoke in a sweet mocking way. "Oh, by the way dear, I am not exactly the person you thought I was. You see, I was somewhat a daddy's girl, if you know what I mean. He and I, well, we redefined the father daughter relationship, somewhat. No, Ruth. I cannot tell him. It is all I can do to face this battle that is before me."

"That is why you moost tell him. He can help you."

"Only God can help me now. You heard what the doctor said. I can't tell him I am carrying some perverted criminal's child. Every time he would look at me, he would hate me a little more. By the time this child was born, I will have driven him away. No, I must be the one to make that choice. I cannot make him the bad guy in this. He has been brave and strong and true. He shouldn't have to make this choice."

"Boot, he has a right to choose."

"I can never face him again."

"Tell him, Lamby."

"How? How do I tell him that when he married me, his wife was used and spoiled? How do I tell him that I cannot offer him a pureness in which he deserves?"

"Joost like you told me, Lamby," the old woman pleaded.

"I can't. I have to tell him that he can never have one hundred percent of me? There will always be that part of me that is dead and festered, rotted from the touch of my own dad and brother? And if that is not enough to putrefy him…" She couldn't finish, because the thought was too hideous. Cold chills crept across her.

182

Inevitable Grace

She did not know, that on the other side of the open door, her husband sat in shock, guilt, and hatred. His heart cried out to his wife. "But you have told me, and I love you even more. I want to keep you safe from all harm. I want you, only you, in any condition in which I can have you. Oh, Grace, I am so ashamed. I let you down, when you needed me most. It is my fault you have to suffer for the rest of your life with this child. I am not brave, strong, or true. If I had been a man, I would have found you, before all this happened. Can you ever look at me again without seeing what a coward I am?"

It was more than his ears could stand. He jumped from his chair and fled.

"What doo ya intend to do?" Ruth continued.

"I must finish the battle which began, when I was a child. I would rather give my life than travel this road, but travel down this road, I must. You understand? Please take care of the girls. One thing about this whole day in which I am thankful, Michelle is finally safe, and her trial is won."

"Lamby, there moost be soom oother way. You are

leaving?"

Grace found it hard to look into her surrogate mother's eyes.
"If we never meet again, this side of heaven, I want you to know
how much I love you. I don't know why God took my own
mother when I was young, but I know he gave me the best
substitute in the world. You have been so good to me. I shall
never forget your kindness."

Ruth's words were choked back by the urge to cry. Lamby
made it sound so final. Of course, she would come back. The
girls needed her, the Laddie needed her, and she needed her.
"Lamby, don't do this. You are making the wrong choice."

"It is the only choice. Please, cover for me."

The invalid slid into her clothes and prepared to leave.
"Thank you for everything." She sealed it with a kiss. Before
Ruth knew what was happening, Grace was gone.

She was left alone to face a family of loved ones with this
news. She did not begrudge Grace, for she knew Grace was
right. Still, she did not want this task before her.

She stepped out to tell the husband, but he was gone too.
Maybe, she thought, he had followed his wife. She hoped so,
anyway.

Amy was not surprised that her mother was not coming home. She remembered her talk with her mom at lunch yesterday, and had already talked it over and helped in making Michelle understand. However, the others were thrown, for Travis did not return either.

Grace made one last phone call to her beloved home. She prayed that Ruth would be the one to answer. "Yes? Ooh Lamby, you have changed your mind?"

"No. I just wanted to make sure the girls were safe and sound before I left."

Ruth became anxious, "No, they are not. Since you und the Laddie have left, they are anything but safe."

"Where is Travis?"

"I doon't know. He left the hospital before you, and no one saw him after."

"Well, he can come home, now. See, I was right about him not being able to look at me with this thing in me. If he calls, you may tell him that I shall not bother him anymore. Goodbye dearest Ruth."

"Lamby, don't…" She heard the dial tone. Grace had hung

up. "Doggone that Lamby. She's stooburn as a mule."

Grace went to the bank and withdrew her meager savings. To her surprise, Mr. Jameston had reimbursed every payment she had made toward Michelle's bail, so there was enough to buy a plane ticket.

At the airport, she made the call to Ruth and then to Shawn to announce her coming. She had surpassed her twenty-four hours, and, of course, he made his usual threats but was appeased to hear that she was on her way now.

When Grace loaded the plane, she said goodbye to her old life, expecting to never be able to return home again. She sadly boarded and looked back one last time. "Goodbye Springfield."

Past Grace

Grace carried only one bag down that long lonely drive. The years faded between the last time she traveled this road and now. She remembered watching nervously every step she took, as she ran down that road for her life, hoping and praying no one had seen her, some twenty odd years ago. The pounding of her heart reminded her how it had beat wildly all those years ago. She was equally as nervous now. She was purposely walking right back into the nightmare she had fled so desperately.

The old farm had changed a lot, but mostly to become run down with insufficient care. The fences were fallen. The lower pastures were overgrown. The old pond had not been drained in many years. The animals, if there were any more animals, must be in the upper fields. She wondered if they were still running the farm or just living at it. Once upon a time, they owned beautiful horses, beef cattle, not to mention fields of hay and corn. At one point they even owned sheep. There were no ducks and geese on the pond.

Looming, threatening, ahead the old farmhouse eerily greeted the comer. "I have a secret to tell." It seemed to whisper in the wind. The hair on Grace's neck stood on end.

187

"Father, please help me now. I can't do this without Your help." She prayed continually. She had been relieved when Shawn failed to pick her up at the airport. It bought her a few minutes more of peace. Now that the house was so close, Grace began to shake.

She knocked on the door, as a stranger selling products. This would be the hardest part. If she could get through the initial confrontation, she just might be able to pull this off. After a long wait, Shawn opened the door.

"Gracie, it's about time. Finish up the dishes, while I get out of here. I will be back in about an hour. He is upstairs in bed." He handed her the dishtowel, went to his car, and drove away without another word.

Grace For The Broken

Great, now she had to face him alone. She entered the den of the ancient house, and again the years faded. It was almost exactly as it was on the day she left. In front of the brick fireplace was the same old sofa, piled with clothes, the old console TV right where it always stood, and the bar hanging in the kitchen could be seen from the doorway. It naturally was too cluttered to see the beautiful maple wood.

The stench of filthy dishes permeated the air. Grace slowly took off her hat, while looking around. This would be the first task to undertake. The dishes were piled on the counter, on the table, and in the sink. When she was little, she spent most of her time in this old kitchen. The refrigerator was different, but that was the only difference.

She stepped down into the laundry room, where clothes piled could not determine the clean from the dirty. The bathroom to the right was small, but it contained all the original plumbing. As a child these responsibilities frightened her terribly. Grace laughed at the thought of her being scared of such trivial things. It all may appear to be endless, but it wasn't.

Well, this was her life now. No turning back at this point. Grace lay down her meager bag. She searched the refrigerator for something to cook for supper, but ended up going back to the porch to look in the big freezer.

She began a load of clothes and dishes, while working up the courage to climb the steps to face him. She breathed a prayer with every breath. When, at last, it was time to bite the bullet, she took a tray up.

A set of sliding doors separated the den and kitchen from the other side of the house. These used to be the family room and piano/sewing room. There they were the steps, which she slowly ascended. The first and second step creaked under her weight. Memories flooded back. "Heavenly Father, I don't know if I can do this," she mumbled.

His door was open. It was now or never. She must enter.

Her body trembled in sheer fright of the unexpected. It had been a lifetime since she had seen this man last. He had made her tremble as a child, and Grace never imagined she would ever feel that fear again. He had always been so large, towering over her with his sickening voice.

She stepped in and barely whispered, "I made you some soup. Do you feel like eating?"

His eyes lightened and he smiled. His once red hair had

grayed. He looked small and weak to Grace. He definitely was nothing to fear. "My little Gracie. You've come home. Let me look at you. My, you have grown into quite a beautiful young woman. You brought me some soup? You do love me. This is wonderful."

"Will you be able to come down for supper? I am frying up some pork chops, with mashed potatoes and beans."

"I wouldn't miss it for the world. It has been many a year since I've had a good home cooked meal. Let's face it, your brother is no cook."

Grace tried to ignore the trembling limbs. She was not sure what to expect. It seemed as if she was in some sort of dream. It wasn't real. It was time to wake up. "Wake up! Wake up, Grace. It is a beautiful day in Oregon, and Samson is waiting to be fed." She opened her eyes, but the dream refused departure. There stood one of whom she had feared for her entire life.

She quickly left his presence, because she was afraid he would require external emotionalizing. Two loads of clothes had been completed, and three quarters of the dishes had been washed, dried, and put in the proper places. Delicious aromas were beginning to fill the house, and then, Grace was finally able to breathe again.

A Legacy Without Grace

Out of nowhere, a clamor of running and yelling neared the kitchen. Suddenly, at an amazing pace, it stopped abruptly. Grace was facing two dirty-faced children. The girl was petite, wearing raggedy old jeans that looked like they had seen many years, before a whole family moved out of them. She was beautiful underneath all the dirt. Her eyes were violet, like Grace's, but her hair was blond. She reminded Grace of herself, when she was a girl. She looked to be about seven.

The boy was considerably bigger. His clothes were less worn and actually fit, but he was twice as filthy. He had red hair and blue eyes. He had his hands on the girl, as if he were about to drag her to the floor by her throat.

Both looked up at Grace with enlarged eyes. "Who are you?" the girl asked in awe. She was enchanted by the woman before her.

"I am Grace. Who might you two be?" she responded cheerfully.

"I am Angel. This is…"

The boy interrupted rudely, "We live here. Are you going to

be our maid?"

"I most certainly am not. Angel, why do you live here?"

"My daddy owns this house."

Grace stood astounded, "And just who is your dad?"

"His name is Shawn," the boy spoke rudely again. "Question is, what are you doing here?"

"Oh." Grace became excited. This was not something she had counted on, but it was a welcome surprise. "I guess that makes you my niece and nephew."

"We don't got an aunt," the boy sulked.

"You sure are pretty. Are you going to stay with us?"

"I am for a while. Is that alright with you?" Grace gently pulled the fallen strands of golden hair from the girl's face.

"Goodie," said the girl.

"Whatever," said the boy, who then continued to jerk his sister to the floor.

"That is enough of that," Grace said, pulling the boy off

Angel with one hand. He kicked her leg and winced, when she refused to let his collar go. "Young lady, you get in the bathroom and wash your face and hands for supper. You, young man," she pulled him by the collar to the sliding doors, "get upstairs and take a bath. Do not come down until you are clean. If you waste time, you will miss supper."

"You don't tell me what to do. Get your stupid hands off me," he shrugged uselessly to free him from her grip. "I'll tell my daddy."

"You may tell whom you please. Meanwhile, get up those stairs and bathe."

"No. You can't make me."

Grace wasted no words. She loosened the boy's own belt, but did not have to strike him with it. "I will not give you another chance. You get up those steps and into the shower, now!"

For whatever reasons, he obeyed her orders. Yes, he stomped angrily, but heeded, nonetheless. Angel stood in astonishment. No one had ever talked to Ted that way. He certainly had never minded anyone before, not even dad.

Shawn had come in and went immediately up the stairs. Ted

194

was quick to run and tattle on Grace, but sulked again, when his dad ignored him. Supper was on the table, when he came down the stairs again.

"Boy, I'm starved."

Grace walked to Ted and checked behind his ears, and under his arms. "March right back up there and do it again."

"What? Why? I don't have to."

Grace turned away to complete her task. She said her words pleasantly, "If you don't hurry, you will miss all of supper."

Once again, the boy stomped angrily up the stairs, cursing with each step. Angel set the table without even being prompted. The cooking had been her chore for the last year. She was used to cooking and cleaning which made her like her aunt immediately.

All were sitting at the lovely table and partaking of the delicious food, when Ted descended one more time. Grace repeated her scrutiny for dirt, but accepted his cleaning this time.

As he sat down, though, Grace angered him again. "The next time I hear a curse word come from your mouth, young

195

man, I will wash your mouth out with soap. You will get no other warning. We don't say words such as that, and we do not take my Heavenly Father's name in vain."

The boy looked at his dad, then his granddad. "Ain't you going to say nothing to her?"

Shawn looked at his plate, hoping that his dad would reprimand the wayward daughter. The old man smiled with pleasure. He had a home again.

Before going to bed, Shawn visited his dad's room "Dad, you need to do something about her. She can't treat my son that way."

"Son," he pitifully responded. "It had been so long since we had a woman in the house. Give her what she wants. Don't run her off again. That snot nosed spoiled brat of yours could use some discipline, and being that you aren't man enough to do it, let her."

The words stung. How dare he? He had always been faithful to his father. She had not. She left them high and dry. Well, the old man would leave him everything, when he croaked, so he would bide his time.

Grace For The Forsaken

Grace settled into her new life unwillingly and regrettably, yet necessary. She was haunted by the demon of memory, which played torturously as she slept in the same bed as she did when she was a little girl. Loneliness consumed her. The loss of her children, the loss of her husband, and the loss of all that she valued became almost unbearable.

She kept in touch with Ruth who vowed to never mention to anyone that she was in contact. Ruth kept her abreast of all that was going on in Oregon. The news about her husband was what broke her heart the most. It seemed he didn't care if she ever came home. He hardly mentioned her any more. With Singleton in prison for his actions, Travis assumed full control over the Sinclair office in Oregon.

The prosecution had so much hard evidence, a trial was unnecessary for Harris and Singleton. Both men made a deal, since Grace's brave actions had sealed their fate without question.

All the children had been returned to their rightful homes. So Grace's home affairs were wrapped neatly up, and they no longer needed her. It was one thing to not be wanted by one's husband, but to not be needed by your children hurt in a whole

197

new way.

One night Angel hid inside the huge boxwood bush beside the driveway. Grace remember the old hiding place. It had been her refuge many times. Why was that little girl hiding there? What must she have endured?

Grace wondered since having come here. She had hoped beyond hope that old habits had died, but from the expression on Angel's face, that hope was in vain. Fear would not allow the child to explain her tears, but Grace knew. Grace would become that little girl's rescuer.

She introduced the children to church, which Ted bucked profusely. He wanted nothing to do with this aunt that made him obey rules. He took every opportunity to embarrass her, but his aunt did not seem to embarrass so easily. Nonetheless, Ted was gaining knowledge of the Truth. On the other hand, Angel fell in love with the greatest love story ever told.

After the initial fears had been squelched, Grace found living in her past terror bearable. It was so different, facing the boogey man as an adult. As a child, everything seems larger than life. As an adult, she was unable to find a reason to be scared.

One thing that changed Grace's attitude toward her dreaded

task was her daily reading of the Word. There, she found Comfort, but she also found things she didn't want to find. God said to love those that hate you, and pray for those that persecute you. Lesson number one: She had to learn to love the two people she despised the most. Love thy enemies. How can you love someone who hurt you as much as these two had, which brought up lesson two: Forgive all. She had to somehow, forgive them, which meant, never to be remembered anymore. How do you forget, when you face the scars every day? These were near impossible requirements. Pray for those that persecute you. That, she could do. Praying was something she had always depended on.

Prayer is what actually helped her through each day. Had it not been for the intervening Hand, she would have never been able to accomplish that which was required of her. So, each day, she lived before these people as unto the Lord.

Cooking, cleaning, and running the old farm kept Grace more than busy. She had little time to dwell in the past. However, as she lay on her bed from years gone by, the demon of memories began haunting her again. They began tearing at her sanity. The only thing that kept the woman alive and willing to wake up every morning was the need to keep her niece safe from harm.

After the first few months, Grace was unable to hide the enlarging belly any more. The secret about her pregnancy was out. There was not much Shawn or her dad could do about it, so they ignored it.

Grace still kept in private contact with Ruth by letter mostly. From the beloved Scotswoman's correspondence, it appeared that Travis was happy and content with having her gone. She didn't know if she could ever go home to face his hurt eyes. He could not look at her at the hospital, and still, after time had passed, he wanted no part of her shame. It was a good thing the old man had not died. Grace didn't know where else she would go. Her husband had made it obvious, she could not go home.

She would have to decide if she'd be able to raise this bastard child? Could she get past the evil conception and learn to love it as she should? Could she part with it, and adopt it out? If that was a possibility, could she face the consequences years from now?

Redeeming The Graceless

One day, late in her seventh month of conception, Grace was summoned to the bedside of the dying man. For several weeks now, he had been bound to his bed, unable to get up for the simplest bodily functions. Grace had tended him gently.

"Yes," she spoke softly. "What is it? Are you in pain?"

"Yes, but not the kind you are thinking. Little Grace you have given up your own life to come here and nurse me these last months." His words were difficult to say, while he struggled slightly to breathe. "I know what it cost you, especially since you and your husband are expecting a new child. I think you should go home to him. Shawn will take care of everything here."

"That is kind of you to release me, but I'll not leave until I have concluded my duties here. This baby is going nowhere for a while yet."

Grace wanted to withdraw her hand from his, when he took it, but something was different in his touch. "I have watched you, little Gracie. You have something real. I don't understand why you don't hate my guts. I have done some despicable things to you for which I am truly sorry. I can only beg your forgiveness."

Grace could not look at him. This was number one, hands down the hardest thing ever asked of her. Here was the devil incarnate, on his deathbed, begging for redemption. Was she supposed to just forget all the years of torment? Was she to forget the vile breath and putrefying touch? Was she supposed to smile and act as if nothing had ever happened? According to the Word of God, the answer to all of the above is yes. When Christ forgives us, it is never to be remembered against us again. Only Satan remembers. Christ had forgiven her for much. She should be Christ like and forgive also. She whispered, "You are forgiven."

"No Grace," he placed a restraining hand on her arm, as she prepared to be leave. "Don't go. I need absolution. I haven't much time left. Tell me how to get it, please."

"What is it you want me to get you?"

"Your God, does He forgive as easily as you? Could He ever love me, after the abominable things I've done?"

"God sent His Son to seek and to save those that which is lost. *For God so loved the world that He gave His only begotten Son, that whosoever believeth in Him should not perish, but have everlasting life.* You are a 'whosoever'. He sent His Son to pay your sin debt and mine. He promises that, *If we confess our sins, He is faithful and just to forgive us our sins, and cleanse us from ALL unrighteousness.* He did it for whosoever."

"All I have to do is tell Him what I have done? It sounds too simple. Will I go to heaven, if I do that? I can feel the flames of hell pulling me toward death. I don't want to go to hell. You have shown me a better way since you've come. What must I do to go to heaven?"

"You can do nothing. It has been done for you already. Christ paid the price for your sin. All you have to do is accept His sacrifice of salvation for you. It is that simple. He said we must come with childlike faith."

"I do accept His sacrifice. I don't want to go to that awful place."

Grace continued to explain, "*For whosoever calleth upon the name of the Lord shall be saved. It is by faith, not by works, lest any man should boast.* You see, it is nothing that we could do, only the faith in He who gave all."

"How do I ask him?"

203

"You simply ask. He said, '*If thou shalt confess with thy mouth the Lord Jesus, and shalt believe in thine heart that God hath raised him from the dead, thou shalt be saved. For with the heart man believeth unto righteousness: and with the mouth confession is made unto salvation.*' You must acknowledge that you are a sinner. It has to be your choice."

The old man lay at the door of death, when he gave his heart to Christ. At least he accepted this side of the door, because that night, before the bedtime hour, he uttered his last words. "Gracie, there is something I must tell you, before I go. It is about your mother." His breathing was labored and challenging. "Your mother, she…didn't…" with that incomplete confession, he drew his last breath.

It was different, than when Isaiah died in her arms. Isaiah was the father she never had. The man before her, now, was a complete stranger. What was he going to tell her about her mother? Her dear precious, beautiful mother.

At least that demon was dead and buried. This one would never be able to haunt her again. Shawn had been gone for about a week, and Grace had no clue to where he was, so she proceeded with the funeral on her own. The sad pathetic truth was that only Grace, Ted, Angel, and the preacher of the little old country church she loved so much, were the only people at the old man's funeral. It was a fitting result of the way he lived. The wind blew flakes of snow with a cold bitter vengeance. He was buried on Christmas Eve, and the snow seemed to be a metaphor for the way he died. As Christ washed his sins white as snow, the snow washed the memories of evil from Grace.

Grace For A Sloth

Grace appreciated the time alone with her niece and nephew. She was able to instill some important values and morals without the contradiction of her brother. Another week passed, and she still did not see him. She was secretly thrilled that he had not come back to destroy the contented happiness that Angel seemed to gain during his absence.

Since coming, Grace dressed Angel in completely new attire. She no longer wore the hand-me-downs belonging to Ted. The child wore pretty dresses, which actually fit properly. Grace even bought the girl a pair of patent leather shoes after she begged for them.

Ted already had the best clothes, because his dad favored the son, but she did buy him a Bible. Daily, she read the truths from the Word to them. They were being educated in an entirely new way. Ted had already begun to show signs of being subdued. He had learned to treat his sister like he would like to be treated himself in the eight months Grace had come to stay. He didn't like it. Sometimes, the old habits would send him into remission.

Grace brought in the New Year cleaning out all the old man's clothes and personal belongings and packed them away. She would take them to Goodwill, after she made sure Shawn did not want anything from them. The old man's room showed no signs of ever having been occupied. True to character, Satan wanted to keep throwing up the haunting memories in which that room held.

Shawn came dragging in two weeks after the old man died. He was fit to be tied. Whatever problems he was running from, he was not willing to share. The only emotion he showed toward his father's death was relief. He did not even mind that he had been absent from the funeral. He made a comment on how all that money would come to him now. Whatever his reasons seemed to be, he had imagined that his sister would just stay with him, cook, clean, and be in servitude to him and his children. He even reiterated his threat to keep her there.

The only reason she stayed on was for the sake of Angel and Ted. A new fear came into Angel's eyes. She should be less afraid, now that Grace was here, but it did not seem to be enough anymore. Since the father died, the son assumed to revert to his old nasty nature. As a matter of fact, the only reason he had hesitated before, was because the old man held the purse strings. Shawn tightened the reigns on his sister. He hung around all day, refusing to go anywhere, or to let her go.

The children went to school and came home. If they needed something at the store, he would escort her. He was afraid that she would leave, now that the old man was dead.

Shawn did nothing in the way of work. He demanded more from the three that sometimes seemed possible to deliver. Grace worked from morning to afternoon outside, working on the tractor or other farm equipment. Yet, every day, she was expected to have a meal on the table three times a day, without fail. Grace contemplated leaving, but it only took one look into Angel's eyes to make her change her mind.

Caught With No Grace

This went on for only a week, before the Lord intervened. Grace was, physically, in no condition to protest too much. She was nearing delivery time, and it rendered her less able to fight. But she did not think far enough ahead to wonder about her due date, so God took action in His perfect way.

Like a dog that goes back to his own vomit, Shawn went back to his own nature-defying crimes. The lust for liquor consumed him and dictated most of his actions. He became abusive verbally. One time he raised his hand, as if he was going to strike his sister, but there was something in the fire in her eyes that held his hand back.

Grace caught him one time slapping Ted, but when she tried to stop the incident, Ted flew into her in a rage. "I don't need you. Leave me alone," he had yelled at her. On the other hand, Grace had never seen Shawn raise even his voice at Angel.

No, it was not that kind of abuse that the little girl suffered. For her, it was a harsher and crueler kind of abuse, but the Savior sent an earthly savior to help the child.

It occurred one day, when Angel was sent to do her daily chores. This included feeding the cows and filling the tubs with water. The once great Angus herd had diminished into only fifteen, and it only took a few minutes to do. Grace had exercised the one horse earlier and fed her, so Angel was relieved of that chore.

Grace was working on supper, while Ted and his dad were off who knows where. Grace was just putting the potatoes on to boil, when a sharp pain brought her to attention. She couldn't figure it out. It did not feel like a pregnancy pain. It was familiar. It was not until Grace saw Ted cross the back yard in a sullen fit that it dawned on her what was going on.

She made a quick stop before swiftly making her way to the barn. She silently approached. At first, she was not sure she had the strength, but then, her Father took the burden.

"Get up!" she spoke disgustedly.

Turning abruptly into the two barrels of his own shotgun, Shawn snarled, "Get out of here. This isn't any of you business," he turned to continue.

"I'll not repeat myself," she insisted.

He raged in a drunken stagger. "I'll tend to you later. Now, leave me alone."

"You lay one more hand on that girl, and I will blow your head off." When the first shot landed between his feet, he realized she meant business and he straightened in an attempt to reprimand her. Grace continued looking down the barrel of the gun, "Now, Angel go to the house and call the police. Dial 911, and they will send someone quickly." To Shawn, she ordered, "Get your hands on your head an keep them there."

"Can't I put my clothes back on?" he tried to overcome.

"No. Get your hands in the air. Don't move a muscle."

Although he tried to lighten the situation by talking his way out of it, Grace said nothing. She waited patiently for the police to arrive. Indeed, it was a little while before they came. Meanwhile, Angel had run back behind Grace. She peered from behind the aunt's back at the animal she called Daddy.

"Come on Grace. You're scaring my daughter. Put down the gun."

"I am not the one scaring your child." When Grace heard the sirens, she sent Angel to direct them to the barn.

Ted also heard and came running. He knew nothing of what was going on. The first two officers had emerged and were coming toward the barn, when the boy pushed past. Upon spying the gun pointed at his dad, the boy savagely tackled the gun bearer, knocking her hard on the ground.

"Hold up little man." One officer pulled the attacker up by the collar.

"Get your hands off me."

Shawn was busy clothing himself again, quickly, during the altercation, but not quick enough for the second policeman to note the facts.

The officer gently lifted Grace to her feet. "Are you okay ma'am?"

"I think so," she replied, while holding her womb carefully. In the other officer's grip, the boy still fought for his freedom.

"Are you sure? We have an ambulance on the way. What's going on here? Is this some sort of family dispute?"

"No sir. It is not." She put her hand on Angel's shoulder, as the girl tried to rub her belly to comfort the baby. "I want this man arrested for raping and molesting his eight-year-old daughter, here."

"You're crazy Grace. Is that what you think was happening? No wonder you were so mad at me. I wasn't raping my child."

212

She ignored his protests and continued, "It has happened before, but I could not prove it. This time, I walked in, catching him in the act."

The officer looked into the terrified eyes of the little victim. They needed no words to know the truth, but they had to do it all by the book. "What is your name, little one?"

Angel fairly climbed underneath Grace's dress. Grace faced her, kneeling. "It is safe. He cannot hurt you anymore, if you don't let him. You have to tell the truth, so they can stop him." The girl remained silent. Grace spoke to the officer again, "Will you take him out of here? She is frightened of him. You cannot question her around the perpetrator."

They were all ushered into two separate squad cars, since the second one had arrived meantime. Ted pitched a fit and ranted and raved from the front seat, cursing Grace for her betrayal.

The trip to the police station lasted all night and most of the next day. The court appointed a doctor to examine Angel, and the truth had been revealed. Although, he denied it to the end, he had left solid, undeniable physical proof of his sins. In the end, it was decided by the lawyers and judge that there would be no need for a trial, because of the overwhelming proof, plus the testimony that Grace was able to expel from the child victim.

Bestowing Grace

The return to the old house was triumphant. Shawn Sorenson was sentenced to fifteen years in prison. Had the judge known about his past crimes, he would probably have gotten close to life. As it was, he would be locked away for a while; that is, if no one killed him in prison first. Criminals were guilty of a lot of crimes, but they all had a special hatred toward child molesters. If he ever made it back from prison, all visits to his children would be supervised. He would never get the opportunity to hurt either one again.

The whole ordeal was completed with as little discretion as possible. One unexpected turn of events that occurred was that the whole Sorenson farm and fortune had been bequeathed to Grace solely. It was the last thing in the world she had expected to happen, but the old man felt Shawn had received his, while he was alive.

Grace was unhappy about this decision. She was laden with material things of a world in which she wanted no part. Add two children with a need for a lot of help to the mixture, and Grace was showing signs of exhaustion. The last eight months had drained her both mentally and physically.

Shawn had divorced his second wife, and after stealing his

children, she disappeared completely. Grace wasn't quick to judge a mother for leaving her children like that. A person would have a reasonable excuse for doing so. One could only imagine what Shawn had done to this poor woman to leave her children in this manner.

So, while Grace hired an investigator to find the missing mom over the next few weeks, she pulled together the final transactions necessary for moving on with her life. There was so much to be done within such a short time. Grace wanted all her t's crossed and i's dotted before her due date.

It did not take long for him to find the remarried woman, so Grace, Ted, and Angel made the trip to Vermont. Snow had already covered the beautiful greenery. The rental car slid occasionally in the snowy road, but the trip was finally complete. They were all nervous about meeting this new woman, Ted, most of all. He still did not know if he could ever learn to behave the way Aunt Grace had taught him.

The answer to Grace's knock was a fairly handsome man. After explaining who she was, and the purpose of her visit, he led Grace into the warm, comfortable home. It had the essence of a comfortable income, and a great show of elegant taste. They were seated on an antiquated couch, appearing to have come out of the nineteenth century. Grace gave the look to the children that seemed to say, "Be on your best behavior. This is expensive, and if you destroy, I will whip hard," so they both sat erect and straight.

The man that invited them in called to another room, "Angela! There is someone to see you."

Presently, a middle-aged version of Angel appeared in a doorway wiping her hands on an apron. She stopped all action midway. Upon seeing her children, the woman burst into tears and wrapped them in her arms. "My babies! You brought me my babies. Who are you? How are you two? Oh, how I've missed you so much. I can't believe you're here." She was eying Grace warily. She had a resemblance to her first husband's father and felt an immediate uneasiness about the woman because of this.

Angel burst forth, unable to keep her calm anymore. "This is Aunt Grace. She's been taking care of us. She's really nice, mom. You will like her bunches. She's made things better for everybody."

The woman looked cautiously at Grace. Any relation to her ex-husband had to be rotten to the core. She became frightened again. What did she want?

Nonetheless, Grace had a smile that would charm anyone.

Her voice was gentle and kind. It only took one word for the woman to fall under her spell. "Hello. It is nice to meet you. Please, call me Grace."

"Angela," the woman responded to the outstretched hand.

"We had a little trouble finding you. You made a thorough job of disappearing. We have been trying to find you for several days."

"Not to be rude, but why have you come? Don't take me wrong, but your brother was a cruel, vicious man. He took my children from me and threatened to have me put away, if I didn't leave and never come back. Now, you are here, with them. Are you here to torment me more?"

"No, mommy. Don't you want us to live with you?" Angel asked almost in tears.

Angela looked at her child in surprise. "What do you mean live with me? Of course, I would love nothing better."

"Mrs. Shelby, I mean Angela, a few things have occurred in the last few months. The children have been through numerous changes. First, their grandfather died last month." Grace could tell from the woman's expression that there was no love lost between the two. "The other huge change in their life is that

217

their father is serving a long sentence in prison. Correct me if I am wrong, but you are the children's mother. It was assumed that you would want to raise them."

The woman could no longer fight the tears. She engulfed Angel, but a sulking Ted recoiled her touch, mumbling something under his breath.

Grace continued, "May I speak with you alone?"

Ray Shelby took the hint. "Come on kids, I'll make some hot cocoa. You can put the marshmallows in for me." The children followed immediately, per Grace's look.

The woman looked fearfully at Grace, afraid to hear what the other woman was about to say. Grace began, "Shawn is in for child molestation. Angel will need a lot of help with this. It is crucial that she seeks Christian counsel. It has matured her beyond her years, but I am afraid that it had affected Ted in a negative manner, more so than Angel. He has learned many behaviors that need to be reversed. He has done a lot to obtain his father's attention, but little captured it. He is much needier."

The woman gasped, "I wouldn't put anything passed that man. Thank you for helping them. I am so grateful to you for bringing my babies from that horror. What do I do when he gets out of prison?"

"He is in for fifteen years. I will be at every parole hearing I can possibly attend. By the time he is released, the children should be of age. I think you will not have any problems as far as that goes."

"It is too good to be true. How can I ever thank you for what you've done?"

Grace answered, as she stood to take her leave. "Take care of them and make sure they get the necessary help. They are yours to love and take care of." Grace was at the door, when she turned again, holding out a small pouch. "This is very little compared to what is owed them, but it is all the free cash left from their grandfather's estate. I am aware that one cannot put a price on the immeasurability of a living being, but I pray this will suffice. Please tell them that I will hopefully see them at Thanksgiving this year. Keep in touch with us."

Tears To Laughter Through Grace

Once she arrived back at the old farmhouse, Grace contacted Mr. Jameston, who agreed to meet with her toward the end of the week. Meanwhile, Grace busied herself with finding a lawyer, and readying the farmhouse for her departure.

She realized she could no longer stay at the place that held so many haunts for her. The demon, memory, had pushed her to the limit of sanity, as it was. She felt that if she stayed much longer, she would be forever lost in that world. She was not concerned about where she could go from here. She simply wanted to get away from here.

She made a call to Oregon, one day, when she knew all would be gone except Ruth in order to find how things were going with Amy and Michelle. She thrilled at the sweet Scottish voice.

"It is so good to hear your voice, my dear sweet Ruth. How are my girls?"

"Land's sake Lamby, I'll be! They are good, boot, they miss the moother. So doos Laddie."

Grace sighed, "Come now, Ruth, He couldn't miss me too much. I would like to see them. Things are in a condition here, in which I am able to see them, safely. Do you think you could talk to my husband and make the arrangements? I will pay for them to meet me anywhere."

"It's doon. I'll speak to 'em tonight."

"Wonderful. My dear friend, how are you doing? You sound tired. Are you getting enough rest? Are they letting you off enough?"

"Oof course." Ruth wanted to keep Grace on the phone for a few more minutes. She knew Laddie would be home, giving him the opportunity to do the right thing and talk to Grace. "Ooh, Lamby, your aunt called two days ago. I'm sorry, boot, it's bad news about your grandmoother. She's gone, Lamby. She fell asleep and never woke oop."

"I suppose that would be the best way. I would love to know I lived my life according to God's will, that when my time came, it would be in my sleep. It'll probably be by a bullet, though. I have days which I wished the cancer had taken me on." She was more thinking aloud, than talking to Ruth. "Never mind that. I'll call Aunt Janet. Thank you for telling me. Ruth, I must go. Please discuss with the girls about one

221

more visitation. I'll call just as quickly as I can."

"Boot Lamby, hold on. The Laddie will be home any minute. You can talk to him."

"Ruth, I do not… has Travis asked anything about me since I left? Has he questioned about where I was, or how I was doing? Tell me, honestly."

She was slow to answer, "Not that I recall."

"Then dear sweet Ruth, what in the world makes you believe he would want to talk to me now? I love him, but he would never be able to look at me again with all my indiscretions. I don't blame him. Tell him I plan on setting him free. He'll not be bound to me."

"Boot Lamby, you don't oonderstand."

"Goodbye Ruth. I will call you again, as soon as I can manage. If I never see you this side of heaven, I want you to know, I'll be standing with our beloved Isaiah and our wonderful Savior to meet you by the River. I love you." Grace quickly hung up for fear of revealing too much of her broken heart to Ruth.

Ruth was no fool. She had not lived with this girl for all

these years and not know her thoughts and actions, even before Grace did sometimes.

Grace took a few minutes to shake off her Oregon mode. She must not think of that world at all. It was beyond her reach. She could never have her happy life back again. Ron Singleton stole every bit from her in one cruel moment. Her life was shattered from one minute choice. She told Amy one time, that if you love someone, you would die for them, like Christ died for a world of sinners. Salvation is not based on works, but should love be defined by the amount of life you give for your child, then Grace had certainly proven her love.

Now would come the time for her to say goodbye to them. She would not drag them through the yo-yo world of being there in an on-off relationship. She would make one final visit, and then forever leave them alone. Travis did a wonderful job at raising Wendy. He'd do an equally great job raising Amy and Michelle.

Travis…now there was a name that physically hurt to think about. Her love had not diminished one iota for her husband. If anything, absence had made the heart grow fonder. He was the deciding factor in all her plans. If he could ever love her again, after this, she could never ask him to raise a rapist's child as his own. It was not only cruel, but also unfair.

Finding Glory In Grace

Grace called to find that the plan for her grandmother's funeral was the following day at eleven o'clock. That would give her time to get back for her meeting with Mr. Jameston in the afternoon. She slept one last night in the childhood house. She fell asleep thinking how wonderful it would be to set fire to this old haunt and watch the flames devour the demons forever.

A threatening sky greeted the new day. It was not raining or snowing, but the wind blew coldly, gripping anything that came in its path. Grace looked like a picture when she departed that morning. She wore a soft cape, being that she could no longer fit in her coat. The cape barely covered her very pregnant stomach, where a little tike was kicking up a storm. This pregnancy had been hard from the beginning. Grace had been sick to her stomach the entire time, mostly from thinking about the evil conception of this cursed thing. How could she ever love this child?

She opted not to carry a purse, so she put her necessities in the inner pocket of the cape and shut the door behind her with a sigh. It was almost over. She put her sleek black leather gloves on, while waiting for the car to warm up. She could almost feel the wind blowing into the car.

The biting winds hurried the service. Grace assumed this was an answer to prayer. She was in no mood to answer the questions of all her inquisitive relatives, and to her relief, none lingered afterward. The tears on Grace's cheek felt like they had frozen in place.

She had many memories of her Grandmother, but few were happy. Grandmother always said she was saved, but she had been a miserable person. She always seemed unhappy and complaining. Grace had to push all these aside to try and remember something pleasant about the deceased.

She began wondering if she, Grace Sorenson Winston, was even capable of love. Was there anyone that she loved unconditionally? It seemed that all she could see was the bad in everyone lately. Had she totally thrown herself into the side of evil? If so, how? She loved God and had always yearned to serve Him. He had walked closely with her, and had helped her more than words could ever say. How could she so thoroughly stray from His will?

Back at the farm, she prepared a simple lunch for Mr. Jameston and then drove to the airport two towns away to pick him up from his flight.

Graceful Tidings

Albert Jameston overlooked the short white haired lady in the black cape. He had not seen her, since her hair had changed color. She had been a petite red head, the last time he saw her. Grace fell on his neck with tears of joy.

"Mr. Jameston. It is so good to see you. It has been so very long. How are you?"

"Grace?"

"Yes."

He played with her hair between his fingers. "What have you done? I loved your red hair."

Grace laughed. It was the first time she had really laughed in months. "I suppose God has a sense of humor. It is His act, not mine."

"My, my. You have changed. Let me look at you. When are you due?"

"Two weeks. Although, it flip flops around in there so much, it would not surprise me, if it came sooner. How is Mrs. Jameston?"

"She is well. Let me get my bags, and we'll go. You can explain to me why you disappeared without a word for all this time. I have been worried about you. Renee has been worried about you. We have all been worried."

The hour's journey gave them time to catch up with all that had taken place in the last months, since Grace had left. She explained as little as was necessary of her stay in North Carolina to satisfy Jameston's questions, but he was not satisfied.

They ate the small lunch. Jameston wiped the final crumb from his mouth. "This was delectable, Grace, but I am sure you did not call me all the way down here for a lunch date. Don't keep me in suspense any longer. I am dying of curiosity."

"How about a walk, while I explain?" she asked cryptically.

At the door, he helped her into her cape. "Are you sure you sure you are up to it? I don't want you to overdo it."

"I am fine, thank you." They walked into the back yard first. "This is the old barn. It is nothing more than a glorified shed, but it has always served its purpose. Most of the equipment is stored here. Over here you have the baler and rake, the mower, the scrape blade, the bush hog, and others. If you were to go further over that hill, you will find two rolling pastures equaling around twenty acres. There are enough blackberries to harvest

227

annually to live on." They walked back toward the house, as she gestured here and there. There is a corncrib behind the barn, as well as another one next to the new barn. We have always produced our own hay and corn. I can show you later where. Down here," they were going to the left of the house now, preparing to climb a hill. "You will see a spring house. The spring runs right through it. It is perfect for keeping watermelons in to get cold. Also, in the pasture behind it are some beehives. Honey and the walnuts those trees produce were always sufficient to see us through another year. We always drained the pond every year. It is stocked with trout."

"That is a huge willow tree. Does the row boat still work?" Mr. Jameston asked, as he helped her cross the electric fence.

"As far as I know. I learned to swim and fish in that pond. Now, we are coming upon the new barn. I call it new, because it was the last addition to the place, before I left. My dad and I built this thing pretty much by ourselves. It is in perfect shape. We spent the last summer making any repairs to barn that we could find. You can see that acre at the edge of the land over there that was the garden. It yields fruitful every year. Here is the tractor. It may be a few years old, but I assure you, it was taken care of. All together, you are looking at over seventy-five acres of land. The cattle and horses, pigs and chickens, geese, ducks, and all the animals are running scarce right now, but we can always build them back up again."

"Grace, this is all glorious, but I don't seem to understand what you are wanting from me. You know you can ask me anything. I will give it to you, if I have it."

Grace laughed, "It is not like that, sir. I want to donate this place to help other children. I want to give it to you for another location for your foundation."

Acceptance of Grace

"I know it is close to Virginia, but it could be self-sufficient. You could run it at an even break, if you wanted to. There is plenty for the children to do, and there is plenty of room to build what you need. It is yours." She pulled her hands from the inside of her cape. "Here are the papers. All we have to do is and have you sign them. If you do not want it for this purpose, then it is yours to do with as you wish."

It was minutes before the man could bring his voice to his command. They were in the warmth of the barn. The wind, at least, was not penetrating their clothing. "Grace, this is too much. I do not know what to say. It is awesome."

"Say yes."

"Are you going back to Oregon now?"

Grace lowered her head. "My plans do not include the possibility of ever returning to that life. Too many things have come to pass that prevent me from it."

"Am I to assume you will be staying here?"

"No sir. I will be going far away. I will probably not be seeing you again. The only thing I ask is that you plan and build a new house and burn down the old one. I would never want a child to received possession of one of its demons."

"If I say yes, can we get in out of this wind?"

"Yes," she laughed again.

"Then, yes. I would be so very honored to accept this place for the next site for our foundation. It is huge. Are you sure you want to give this up? I would be more than happy to buy it from you."

Grace spoke in a tone of far away thought, "No, I could never take a dime from this place. You cannot clean up blood money; no matter how hard you try. On the way back to the airport, we will stop and get all the paperwork signed and sent."

"When we burn it, would you want to be here?" asked the dear old friend.

"That would be nice, but not necessary."

They did not speak much, until they were in the warmth of the house, again. Albert Jameston looked around the old homestead walls, which held no pictures. They were old

231

paneled wood that had recently been shined. Grace ushered him through the sliding doors into the living room.

"I will get the coffee. Excuse me."

Once again, he inspected the surroundings. In the nook beside the doors, were lined trophies. He wandered over to see them more clearly. Shawn Sorenson's name was on all of them. There were piles of blue ribbons with his name, as well. Newspaper articles piled up: basketball, horse shows, track. Shawn must have been into athletics heavily during his youth.

Over the piano in the open adjoining room, hung a large portrait of a beautiful creature, which he automatically knew was Grace's mother. It showed of the ages it had hung in that very spot. Albert took it upon himself to take it from the wall. Grace was in no condition to reach or lift, and he was sure she would not leave such a valuable treasure to be burned. Boxes were packed and addressed for Vermont, and some were addressed to a storage facility. Some were marked to be left for the burning. A stray object, like the picture and trophies was not yet packed.

Wearying of Grace

An old Buster Brown shoebox lay atop of an open box. He had not seen that brand of shoes in years. More out of curiosity of the old box than anything, he lifted the lid. He expected to see an old pair of Hush Puppies. Instead, it was full of old photographs. Some were yellowed with age, while others were black and white, and even more with faded colors. A picture of Grace's mother rested on top. Grace favored her mother, but her mother was even more beautiful. They shared the same unique violet eyes and bone structure, but very little else. They did share the same haunted look in those violet eyes. He looked at the portrait over the piano again. She looked completely happy and content in the portrait, yet the picture, she was different. What happened to her between the two?

The box was filled with hundreds of photos, mostly of Shawn and an older man. He could tell this was Grace's dad, because she favored him more than her mother. He had the red hair. He appeared shorter than Grace's mother, but his eyes were dark and evil looking. He compared the two, and found out that Shawn had his father's eyes. Looking at them, he felt a chill. Pure unadulterated poison is what it was. That is what he saw, when he looked into both sets of eyes.

Toward the bottom, he found a single photo of a little girl. There were no others of Grace's mother and only one of Grace. The red hair was undeniable. How could that tiny little creature stand on those bony little legs? The haunt was already in her eyes, and a fear covered her face.

He jolted at the sound. "I didn't know where to send those. The only one that would have a desire for them is dead. I wanted to keep the one of my mother to give Amy and Michelle, so they can have something of their heritage, but I couldn't separate it from the rest. They belong together."

"Your mother was very beautiful. How old was she, when she died?"

Grace took the picture in her fingers gently. A tear surfaced. "She was twenty-four. She had the softest skin. Her cheeks always blushed naturally. I don't believe I ever saw her wear make-up. She used to sing to me. Her voice sounded as if it floated from heaven on the wings of angels. Then, one day, they took her to the hospital, and she never came home again. A few weeks later she died."

"What was wrong with her?"

"I can't be positive, but I have heard things. When my aunt would get mad at me, she would always make some comment about my mother. I was led to believe that they sent her to a mental hospital. They said she went insane and tried to kill herself. I always assumed that raising me was more than she could bare." Her voice quivered. "She didn't want me, so she checked out."

Albert Jameston had never witnessed a more pitiful sight in his life. Before he could think, he held Grace's head against his chest. She had always been his little girl. He wanted her to know how dearly he loved her. There were tears in his eyes as well, when he pushed her back and forced her to look at him. "Look at me, Grace. You can't take what bitter jealous people said and read it as the gospel. If the mental hospital part was right, then there was a legitimate reason for it. I am sure it had nothing to do with you. Look at me, mental sickness is just that, they are sick in the mind. They cannot control it or heal it without help. At least she tried to get help."

"Then, if that part is true, is it hereditary? Sometimes, I feel I can't take another day of living. I feel the battle. I know it sounds crazy, but I can physically feel the battle in my head, and I am not sure of the outcome. I am losing it fast."

He replaced the top on the box and set it aside. "Now, look here young lady. Enough of this kind of talk. You are looking at old photos, which are bringing up wild imaginations without

235

proof. There is not a bit of truth about you going insane. You are the strongest person I know. Now, how much more packing do you have? Can I help you with anything?"

"What time does your flight leave?"

"Oh that? It does not leave until seven forty-five in the morning. I am yours. Where do we start?"

"Let me see. Let's start upstairs. I believe I packed most of it, but we can double check. We could start in Shawn's room. I am not exactly sure where to store his belongings for the time being."

"Why not send them to him?"

Grace blushed, "I cannot send them to him. He is incarcerated."

He helped her up the stairs. "May I ask why he is in prison? You don't have to answer."

Grace was pleased that the darkness could shield her shame. "He was convicted of child molestation. This was his room. Do you see anything I forgot in this room?"

"What about the dresser?"

Grace searched the drawers again. "All clear."

"What about the furniture? It is old, probably antique."

"Feel free to keep anything you want. What is left after the movers come will be burned with the house, so if there is anything you want in the house, please take it."

Grace took him from room to room in the upstairs floor, except one. It was her old room. As soon as Shawn was gone, she had moved into the spare bedroom and never stepped foot into her old room again. It would serve her good to never step foot in it again. She allowed Mr. Jameston to enter it, but she went in another direction.

Graceful Ghosts

The room was bare save a small bed and chest of drawers. Yet, the room drew him against his will. The tiny girl stepped out of the photo from downstairs and walked to the bed. She sat down and began weeping. The hair on Albert's neck prickled. He walked to the closet. Hidden within its boundaries was a mirror, which once rested on the chest of drawers. The girl jumped from the bed and ran to the closet.

"Oh no. Don't look in there. It's the bad glass. Don't look at it, or you will get in trouble."

Jameston shook away the image. That was the one door he shut behind him. He was beginning to understand why Grace wanted to burn the house. The ghosts were bold.

Grace had most of the work completed. There were a few things downstairs needing packing up, and he was a tremendous help. The main decision to make was what to do with the mother's portrait. Would it be fair for Grace to keep it?

The movers came at three thirty and left a couple hours later. Grace offered Mr. Jameston to stay, but the ghosts had spooked him from accepting. He called from the house to make a reservation, in which Grace drove him after all was done.

Grace said goodbye to the house, the farm, and all the related demons of a hated past. She would never have to set foot on that property again, should she not desire it. She was not sure where she would go from here, but she knew this part was over.

They stopped to sign of the papers before dropping Mr. Jameston at his hotel. Another chapter closed.

She sat there for several minutes. Where to now? She started her ignition and began to drive. She did not know where she was going. She ended her journey at the graveyard, where they buried her grandmother only hours before.

She pulled her cape closer around her, as she walked into the brisk evening air. She wasn't sure why she was here, but she was. The workers had submerged the coffin into the frozen earth and the many flower arrangements had been set around, which the strong wind had dislodged. She straightened them.

She wandered over to where they had buried her dad weeks ago. She was young when her mother died, but she should be able to remember. Where did they bury her mother? Why would she not be buried beside her husband?

Grace sat on a nearby bench, pulling her cape around her securely. "What other secrets were you hiding, old man? What were you going to tell me about my mother?" she said out loud.

"Sometimes buried secrets can only be found through new beginnings." Grace was startled out of her thoughts at the sound of a strange voice. She could not turn around. Something held her attention. She was not afraid, just mesmerized. She could see the illuminating light from behind, and felt a security in the comforting voice.

"Do all things have to be secret?"

"Rarely are things what they seem. Why thinkest thou such thoughts?"

"What thoughts might that be?" Grace knew who the speaker was.

"The Master knows all. Do not attempt to secrete anything from Him. Why do you entertain such folly?"

Grace realized the voice was sent to help her. "I am weary and worn. I want that Peace, that only He can give."

"Then, why do you not ask? The Master will comfort you in His arms, if you ask."

"The adversary has implemented disharmony. There is no comfort in this world. Only with Him can I find comfort."

240

"You ponder evil in your heart. Your way is no way. *Know ye not, that to whom ye yield yourselves servants to obey, His servants ye are to whom ye obey; whether of sin unto death, or of obedience unto righteousness?*"

"I have served Him."

"Do you serve the Master now?"

"His presence is no longer with me."

"Nay, He hath said He would never leave you or forsake you. He cannot lie. Your time has not come, yet."

Grace turned slowly. Curiosity had gotten the best of her. Her eyes beheld a light. It had not shape or form. The thought that came to her mind was this: if the Master is the Light of the world, and his angel shone this bright, how much more brighter was the Master?

"I have nowhere to go. I have no strength left to fight."

"So, then lean on the strength the Master gave you."

"That strength is no longer with me. My strength cannot bear to look at me."

"Why is it that your husband cannot look at you?"

241

Grace dropped her head in shame. "Because I carry a constant reminder of evil inside me. I allowed myself to be careless, and evil rested with me. Now, I bear the illegitimate seeds of what I have sown."

"Do not be afraid. Before your son is born, you will love his father with a renewed love."

"But, could my husband ever love me again?"

"With all his heart."

Family Without Grace

Travis had stayed all night at the hospital with Grace. Through the night, she cried out several times, whether it was fear or pain. He couldn't stand to see her suffer so, but every time he would approach her to comfort or help, she would scrambled from his touch. A look of no recognition was in her eyes. She would beg him not to hurt her and promise to be good. She saw him no better than the fiend that tormented her as a child.

He would retreat to the hall, which seemed to quiet her. It finally came to the point he could no longer force his love on her. He had heard the tape. That evil beast had held her, while threatening her children, Renee's life, and even his life with him not even ten feet away. While she was crying for help, he had not heard, nor felt her need. Grace knew he failed to stop the rape.

He left in a blind guilt, after hearing Grace's words to Ruth. He did not blame her one bit. How could he so blindly bring her into oppression by the people that tortured her as a child? He knew Grace had left home when she was young, but he had never stopped to find out why. He should have known better

243

than to allow her brother to give his bone marrow. What price was Shawn asking? He had made two fatal mistakes in one day.

The Mustang drove him anywhere he wanted to go, because he decided he couldn't face Grace right now. By her own admission, she could not stand him right now. He did not want her to not be able to go to her own home because of him. He would be the one to give her some space and time.

He drove to the familiar hotel, which Grace had stayed at during her radiation treatments. After checking in, he ran his fingers through his hair and washed his face. He would head into work, because there was no telling what would happen when the news of Ron Singleton became known. It was the last place he wanted to be, but he also knew it would help keep his mind off his wife.

All this happened on Saturday morning, and on Wednesday, Travis called the house, praying that Ruth would answer. He wanted to find out if he had given Grace enough time. The old hotel was lonely without his loved ones, and he wanted to go home.

To his delight, it was Ruth's voice calling, "Hullo," on the other end.

"Ruth," he started.

"Laddie, are you cooming home? Since you and Lamby are gone, the children are frantic."

"Where has Grace gone?"

"I doon't know. She left the hospital and I haven't seen her since."

"She didn't tell you where she was going?"

"No, Laddie."

"Ruth, she tells you everything. Are you sure she didn't tell you?"

"I'm sure. All I know is that she told me to tell you to coom home. She woon't bother you no more."

"I will be home after work. Thanks."

Grace left the hospital without going home to get her personal belongings. Well, that was the answer to his question. She had no intention of forgiving him, ever. He had run her out of her own home and from her own children.

No Grace In Blaming

All three children were overjoyed at his homecoming. Though Amy found comfort in his arms, Michelle found her own demons hard to bear. She felt a guilt of her own for Grace's disappearance. All had been well, before she came to live here. Even with Amy's explanation, she felt responsible for what happened between Grace and Travis. Mom's absence was affecting all.

Travis had trouble sleeping. Trying to sleep in their bed without her was nonproductive. Sleep evaded him at all corners. He did not ask Ruth about Grace, because he knew Ruth would not tell anything Grace didn't want her to. He sat back and listened, hoping he would accidentally hear something about her.

Grace left a hole in his heart and life when she left. Without her, life had lost its luster. He had to go on for the sake of the children. He could not see the future months ahead, or how they would turn out, so he took one day at a time, trying to survive with some modicum of sanity. His physical strength began to weaken.

He attended Singleton's hearing with a fear that the man may get off, since Grace had disappeared. He had a secret hope that she would slip in for it, so he could see her one more time. However, he learned that his wife had sent an affidavit that sealed Singleton's fate without a doubt. With the tape found in Grace's office, and the plane full of children, he was doomed to prison. Harris was sentenced to ninety years for his participation in the child slave trade, but Singleton would never get out.

Michelle was able to join the regular school with Amy and settled down into a somewhat normal life. She would give anything to have Grace back, but Travis's love and care had to suffice. No one mentioned her leaving the home. Maybe everyone would forget, and she could stay forever.

Wendy's disregard for Grace returned. She thought little of a woman that would up and leave her dad on the spur of the moment without word of explanation for no reason. She had thought better of Grace than that. Had it not been for Dad having to take care of Grace's responsibilities with these children, she would have gone back home with Brad and Terry. She tried to talk to her dad about Grace's leaving, but he told her it was none of her business, and she did not know what she was talking about. Not only did this woman treat her dad like dirt, she had him thinking he was responsible.

Days passed and then weeks, yet Grace did not call her husband. When it turned into months, Travis considered the idea that she had gone for good. He had chosen this life. Also, this was where Renee was, so he was willing to stay on in Oregon.

Relentless Grace

One day, about five weeks after Singleton was sentenced to prison, Travis found an envelope addressed to Grace from the state penitentiary. He tossed it around in the privacy of the bedroom for several days, before he could no longer stand it. He knew it had to be from Singleton. What did Singleton want with his wife?

Since sleep rarely came for him, Travis opened in at four twenty-two one morning during an attack of insomnia. "You have no way of sending it to her." He reasoned to himself. So, he tore the end and dropped the paper out. It read:

Dear Grace,

How is my baby? I hope you are taking good care of yourself. I would hate to see anything happen to our child. I know I'll not be around for the first few years, but when I get out, I will be there for our child. Please send pictures as you get them, so that I may show them off to my friends.

Thinking of you often,

Ron

The letter almost initiated a stroke. How dare he? How could they let him send his victim a letter? He would go to that confounded prison and kill him with his bare hands. Where was Grace? Why did she not check in? Well, at least, if he did not know how to contact her, Singleton wouldn't know either. How he wished Grace would call him. Did she intentionally try to distress him so? He knew he deserved to lose his wife, but now that she was in danger, she should let him keep her safe.

Right, just like he kept her safe from him the first time? What did he expect to do? He could not even find her. "God," he prayed, "Keep her, where I cannot, please. Please don't let anything more happen to her. I ask You to watch over Grace, wherever she may be. If it be Thy will, will You let her come home again? I know I do not deserve a third chance, but You said if I asked for forgiveness, You would give me another chance. I love her so very much. I miss her. I don't want to live without her. If it be Thy will, I ask these things in my Father's precious holy name, amen."

He decided not to share the letter with Ruth. If the idiot was stupid enough to send another, then he would tell Ruth to keep her eye out and throw them all away. He did, however, keep a closer watch on the girls. Over the following months, several more came, but Travis held them in abeyance.

Each morning the man awoke, the first thought on his mind was the sound of Grace's whisper for help. Frequently, he would play back the recording, which James had given him. There was not a time, when he listened to it, that he did not cry. Singleton had known how to force Grace to do what he ordered. How did things get so mixed up?

He was amazed at how well the girls seemed to be handling the situation. Michelle had shown signs of being disturbed, at first, but that soon faded. Amy never showed any signs of grief. It was almost as if she had expected her mom to leave. He was grateful that God had intervened in that aspect.

Renee carried a small amount of guilt, as she went in daily to Grace's job. She didn't understand the reasons behind her sister-in-law's vanishing act. Unlike her brother, she wasn't too proud to ask Ruth about it. However, she was disappointed about the results. If Ruth knew anything, she was being tightlipped about it. At work, she followed the boss's recorded directions to the letter. The fact that Grace had left these instructions so thoroughly left reason for wondering. Why? Had Grace known she was leaving prior to Singleton's acts?

The sister did not approach the brother about his wife. She worried he would read more into it than was real. She waited for him to open the subject, but he never did.

Grace Full Of Gifts

To the great surprise of everyone, Christmas brought converse and contact from their beloved. A package came by UPS with no return address the day after Christmas. There was no letter filled with much desired information on how she was or where, but instead, simple wrapped gifts for each of the girls and Ruth.

It didn't take much convincing to get dad to allow them to open the gifts immediately. He was secretly excited that she had even contacted them. He didn't mind that she was still angry enough to leave him out. He watched Amy's eyes light up as she pulled out a gold chain bearing a heart locket. The pictures inside of the three daughters, plus the engraving on the back brought forth an added gasp, "Oh how beautiful." It read, *With all my love, Mom.*

Michelle's gift was a Bible. It was beautifully bound in leather. Marking John 3:16, was an envelope. The contents of the envelope thrilled Travis more than Michelle. It meant that his wife would be home again. Inside was a completed application for adoption, ready and waiting for required signatures on their end. The instructions included returning it to Stephanie with the appropriate signatures for finalization.

Wendy hated herself for being completely thrilled with her gift. Somehow, Grace had managed the most fascinating painted portrait of her mother. How she did it, they did not know. Grace seemed to have a way of getting anything she needed.

Ruth opened her gift, but quietly closed it up and carried it to her room without a word. No one seemed interested in hers. Travis watched quietly, but said little. He appeared disinterested in the whole matter. He slipped into the kitchen and watched the happy faces in secret.

Renee received a note with instructions from the sister-in-law. *I have not much to give, except your freedom. Be free from the demons, my friend. Pray that they never come back to haunt you.* Grace's gift to Renee had been hidden, and she finally released their whereabouts to Renee, so that she may destroy that part of her life. Renee found them exactly where Grace told her they were in her study. Taped to the bottom of the box was a match. She was holding a photograph and cassette tape, when her brother came in. Travis could not see the words or the match, but he could see the tear rolling down his sister's cheek.

"What makes you so sad, little sister?" he asked, as he walked up behind her quietly.

Grace Of Friendship

Renee jumped and shuffled the pieces back into the box, but not before her brother could see them. "I am not sad. Does this look like the face of a sad woman?"

"The tears do."

Renee smiled, "No brother dear, these are tears of relief."

Travis pulled the tape from her hand. "Do you mind explaining? I am no fool. I saw the picture. Explain."

"I don't owe you any explanations," she spat angrily. This was her private gift. He had no right to intrude.

He pulled the picture out of the box and up to her face. "I have, here in my hand, a picture of Uncle Robert undressed and standing over you. I want an explanation and do not tell me you don't owe me one."

"I don't. It was a long time ago. He is dead now. Let it go."

"Let what go? Tell me he is not doing what it looks like he is doing?" Her refusal to answer angered him even more.

"Fine, tell me who took the picture, and I will ask them."
Again, she was silent. His physical strength enabled him to take the tape easily and place it in Grace's recorder.

Renee unsuccessfully tried to stop him. She turned her head in shame, as she heard his wicked voice on tape. This was the first time she had heard it. This was the first time she had seen the picture.

Travis was towering over his sister. "Why didn't I know about this? How long did he do this to you? Tell me Renee. Did Mom know?"

"No." Renee's voice was unusually quiet, "She never found out."

"So how long?"

"It only happened a few times. After you moved to Wilmington, we stopped him, and he never came near me again. That is when he moved away."

"Who is we?" He knew the answer to his own question.

"Grace came up with the plan to catch him on camera and tape. She is the one that took the picture and made the recording. It worked because after that, he left me alone."

"My wife knew about this and never told me?"

"Travis, your wife was a true and loyal friend to me. I asked her to keep this secret, which she did. You can't be mad at her for that."

"Maybe not, but I do blame you. You should have told me. That is something you should never have had to deal with yourself. If you had told me, I would've stopped him. What would you have done, if this idea had failed? It would not just have been you in hot water."

"Travis, we were young. We did the only thing we could at the time. You weren't there, and we certainly couldn't tell mom."

He shook his head. "I just can't believe the two of you pulled this off. I cannot believe he had the audacity to do this is our own home." A sudden compassion overwhelmed him, as he pulled his sister into his arms. "Renee, I am so proud of you. I would kill him, if he were not already dead. I am so sorry."

"Big brother, I love you." She nestled in his strong arms. "She'll be back, you know. She loves you so much."

He sighed, "I hope you are right, sis, I hope you are right."

Grace Given Gift

"Laddie, can I speak with you?" Ruth asked, coming in the study.

"Yes ma'am." Renee took the cue to leave and did. "What's up, Ruth?"

"Lamby, she poot in my box soomthing for you. She wasn't sure yoo'd want it."

Travis's heart skipped. She was thinking about him! Maybe she would forgive him still. He graciously exchanged the neatly wrapped gift for a kiss. "Thank you."

She patted his cheek on her way out the door. He eagerly ripped the paper to reveal a gorgeous silver pocket watch. A protruding silhouette of a cross was simply placed to perfection on the cover. The hands glided over an angelic scene. On the inside of the top cover, Grace had it engraved with the words, 'Only God could love you more.'

A neatly folded note had been place inside the box. It read:

I pray, in time, you can forgive me. I shall love you for the rest of this life and throughout eternity.

Grace

He fell back into the chair behind the desk. Full remembrance came rushing back. He could still feel the softness of her lips. The freshness of her hair pleased his nose. Forgive her? There was nothing to forgive.

He listened with a close ear for any hint of the whereabouts of his estranged wife. He suspected Ruth of having full knowledge, and possibly Renee, so he inquired without asking. His patience paid off, when days later, Ruth struck up a conversation with him about his wife.

"Laddie, the Lamby's grandmoother died. It would be good for you to go. The Lamby, she don't sound good. I'm worried aboot her. She didn't sound like herself. They be burying her tomorrow." She said without really betraying Grace. She hoped he would not make her say more.

"Ruth, is she hurt?"

"She didn't say. If you leave tonight, you could be there in time. You take my word for it, Lamby's in a bad way."

Travis thought long and hard, after the woman left. Should he? Is this what God had intended him to do? The last thing he wanted to do was cause more pain for his wife.

He pondered and prayed hard for the right decision. At first, he wasn't sure, because he was unable to procure a flight that night, since all the Sinclair planes were in use, but Something kept nudging him to go. He spent a sleepless night and left early in the morning. It was not a straight flight, and he knew he would probably not make the funeral. At least he knew her general vicinity. He believed he could find her now.

He would never imagine her staying in North Carolina for the last months. She had fled far from that place years ago, but he knew she would come home to bury her grandmother. He spent the first hours, after he landed, calling all the local hotels. None had any listings for Grace Sorenson or Grace Winston.

Could he have called this one wrong? He had been so sure he would find her. Brad and Terry questioned him about Grace. They were glad Travis had come to stay during his visit. Terry even helped the cousin call the hotels.

Late afternoon, Travis became frustrated with his failure. He was about ready to call it quits and go home. In one last desperate attempt to commune with the Holy Spirit, he drove out to the cemetery. Inside his cousin's car, the sun was bright, giving the appearance of an alluring day, but once he stepped out, the biting wind struck him boldly. He remembered the exact place, where he had seen Grace's granddad had been buried, so he began to stroll in that direction.

He pulled the collar of the coat, which his wife had bought him in New York, close around his neck. He was looking toward the ground, but a bright light distracted him. He looked as if in a trance. On the bench ahead, he could see a woman with shoulder length hair that was white as snow. She seemed to be glowing with an iridescent glow. As he drew closer, she appeared to be deep in thought, or converse, yet no one was around her.

Finally, he was close enough to hear the words of the woman. He didn't mean to intrude; only his legs had a mind of their own. It was then that he realized the woman was Grace. He listened to a few words, patiently.

"I have nowhere to go," she was saying aloud. "I have no strength left to fight."

She seemed to be talking to another person, but no one was there. He listened carefully to her sentences in hopes of understanding what was going on.

"That strength is no longer with me. My strength cannot bear to look at me."

She must be sick. She was talking about losing her strength. "Oh God," he prayed, "Please don't let the cancer be back."

Grace never looked so beautiful as she did now. She held her head down gracefully in humility, while the strange brilliant light shimmered from her face

"Because I carry a constant reminder of evil inside me. I allowed myself to be careless, and evil rested with me. Now, I bear the illegitimate seeds of what I have sown."

She looked at him, but did not see him. Her eyes beheld something his could not. He did not know who she was talking to, but he knew it was real to her.

"But, could my husband ever love me again?"

His heart broke. She was referring to him. Could he ever love her? The question was, could she ever love him again? He could no longer withhold his presence. He fell before her on his knees and caressed her hands. "With all his heart," he said in truth.

Miraculous Grace

Through the tears, which had welled up in her eyes, Grace could see the light had taken form. The radiating light wouldn't allow her to make clear the form, but the transformation amazed her. She had watched the angel take form, right before her.

Heretofore, the voice was neither male nor female. Now, it sounded masculine. "Could you ever forgive your husband?" he asked.

"For what have I to forgive him? I am the one that has shamed him." She looked at some lint on her cape. She could not force her eyes to focus on the angel. It seemed too sacred a being to look upon.

"You could never shame me. It is I that has betrayed you. I could have and should have stopped what that man did to you."

"I suppose no one could have stopped that man. The Master had His purpose for it all. I just cannot face the look of shame in his eyes. He is so disappointed in me. I let him down."

Travis searched her face. He was aware that she was still talking to whomever it was she was talking to, when he walked up. "Grace." He placed his warm hand on her cheek to wipe the tear that had finally overflowed to her cheek. "Honey. Look at me. Grace."

And then, as if swept into reality, her eyes focused, and she recognized the man before her. "Travis?" she whispered in a poetic voice. "What…oh my!"

He pleaded with his eyes, "I want you to listen to me. Is that why you left, because you thought I resented you?"

"Isn't that why you left that day in the hospital?"

Travis's face exclaimed his emotion of surprise, "I left, because I thought you wanted me to." Grace began to laugh and was unable to stop.

Travis was not laughing though. "You mean you did not want me to leave?"

"No. I thought you left, because you hated me, since I had allowed this abomination."

He grasped her tightly and threw her face into his breast. "Oh my dear Grace. You didn't allow anything. If anything, I allowed it to happen."

"How do you figure?"

With a big hard swallow, Travis faced his bride to say the hardest thing he ever had to say. "When Singleton…was…doing this to you…I was standing right outside that door. I could have stopped him. You know this, because you heard me and cried for help."

"And you thought I held you responsible for that? I don't know about you, but I feel very foolish. I was afraid to face you, and vice versa."

Travis covered her face in his coat again. "All that doesn't matter now. We can go home and raise our children together. I want you to know, I intend to love this child as much as Amy and Michelle. It may not be biologically mine, but it is part of you. I am this child's dad." He searched for approval.

"It is no wonder I've always loved you. You are so kind and wonderful and marvelous. No child, anywhere, could be more blessed than to have you as their dad."

He helped her to her feet. "Let's get out of this cold."

Homecoming Grace

Travis started the ignition for the heater to warm up. The reconvening of the two souls continued, while waiting for warm air to blow out. "I have missed you," Grace smiled.

"We missed you more." He held his hands to feel the air warming. "I am going to Brad's? You'll come with me?"

"I have to take the rental car back."

He pulled her hand to his breast. He did not want to risk letting her go again, lest something else would prevent them from being together. He hesitantly kissed her fingertips. The gloves had done little to keep her dainty fingers warm.

Nonetheless, he followed her to the rental company, where she returned the car she had been renting since her brother's incarceration. There were cars at the old farm, but she would not touch one dime of that place. She considered it blood money and gave it away, as fast as it came.

"Are you ready? Brad and Terry will be thrilled to see you."

Grace shook her head, "There is nothing I'd love better."

"We can stop by and grab my bags, and then catch a flight

home tonight and be sleeping in our own bed."

"I'm not so sure about leaving tonight. We may need to stay for a few more days."

"I really want to go home. I want to get to my girls. Oh, you will be so surprised at Wendy. She has been working with Renee. Renee says she is doing great," he protested.

"That is wonderful, but I am afraid I must insist on staying put for a few days."

Travis submitted in disappointment, "I will go wherever you want, whenever you want. As long as you are with me, I don't care." Grace pulled her cape off, while breathing with heavy dramatic breaths. The heat had become too much for her. Travis had not realized how pregnant Grace really was, until the cape came off. "Oh…you mean…Is it…time?"

Grace shook her head nervously, "Yes."

"Hold on. I will get you to the hospital in a minute. Can you navigate?"

"I don't want a hospital. I was hoping more for a midwife; only I have not interviewed one yet. I am early. Do you think Terry could possibly deliver? I really do not want a hospital."

Graceful Delivery

"You haven't been to a doctor?"

Grace held her breath through another pain and shook her head.

"That's no good," he scolded. "We can ask Terry." He directed his car toward Brad's house. "I can't believe you have not gone to the doctor. What were you thinking?"

"Can you please scream at me later?"

"I'm sorry. I'm sorry," he repeated, as he slammed on the brakes after almost running a red light. "Hold on. We will be there shortly."

By the time they reached the house, the contractions were seven minutes apart. Terry and Brad greeted them at the door, but when Terry saw Grace she exclaimed, "Travis, why didn't you take her to the hospital? She is in labor."

"She wanted a midwife. Would you be able to fill that position? I know that is not your specialty, but could you manage it?"

"Grace, let us take you to the hospital, please," Terry tempted.

Grace shook her head. "I do not…hee…hee…whoo…wish to have this baby…hee…hee…ooooooh…at the hospital. Whoo…whoo…whoo…I'll do it by myself, if I must."

Almost seven hours later, Grace presented to her husband the baby in her arms. "Isaiah, this is your daddy." The love in her eyes for her husband perfected the moment.

He leaned on the edge of the bed and wrapped his arm around the two. "Hi there Isaiah." He touched the baby's hand, and then kissed Grace. "I dare say, Isaiah, your mom is the most beautiful woman in the world. You are blessed to belong to her."

"You two look as if you are the first person in the world to have a baby," Terry teased, coming back into the room, while drying her hands."

"Thank you Terry." Grace squeezed her hand, when she neared the bed. "You can have new cards made up now: Terry Whitaker - midwife," she laughed.

"Is it safe to come in?" Brad peeped his head in the door.

"Come in and see my son, cousin," Travis said proudly. "Here, would you like to hold him?"

Brad shied away, "That's okay. You keep him, while I look at him."

Terry laughed, "Brad, I do believe you are afraid of a baby. My big he-man, afraid of a baby, now that I can have fun with."

"He sure is big," said the cousin.

"He sure is," agreed his wife. "He is also healthy. You are lucky to have one so healthy, since you have not been to the doctor during your pregnancy."

"Not luck. It is my Lord and Savior watching out for us. He knew what He was doing all along."

"Well, whatever it is, he is a cutie pie. Did we decide on a name?"

Grace smiled, but it was not her normal charming smile. It was different. She wore a peaceful, contented smile. The kind a new mother wears, as she looks upon her firstborn. "Travis Isaiah Winston."

"Oh, I like that." Terry looked warily at Travis. It was just like her cousin-in-law to give that child his last name. Grace was not to blame for the pregnancy, but she shouldn't have given him her husband's name, being that it was not his child.

Brad was less discrete. His voice betrayed his disapproval. "That is good. Well, I better get back in there. You get some rest Grace."

Terry followed suit. "Yes, Travis, she needs rest."

Alone again, Travis looked his wife in the eye. "I love you. Nothing will ever change that. No one will ever change how I feel about this boy."

Grace frowned, "He is your son, Travis."

"I know, and I will always love him as my own," he expressed excitedly.

"No, I mean, he is your son," she insisted.

Travis was stunned at her assertion. "How do you know?"

"Look at him. Tell me you can't see that he is yours."

"You think? We could run a blood test."

"I need no blood test to tell me. Look at Isaiah. This is our son, biologically as well as every other way. God told me so.

You cannot argue that."

"I never dreamed that it was even a possibility."

"No one ever thought twice about it. It was just assumed on every person's mind, even mine."

He embraced his wife and son anew with love he never fathomed he could feel.

Joyous Grace

It was a joyous homecoming. Ruth killed the fatted calf for the prodigal. Amy and Michelle ran excitedly to see their new baby brother which dad presented proudly.

Ruth's eyes filled with tears when she met her husband's namesake. She embraced the child to her bosom, muttering in her rich Scottish, blubbering happily.

While Wendy held aloof, Amy and Michelle refused to let go of mom. After having been without her for eight months, they wanted nothing else but to hold on to her. Grace petted the two girls gently. "I can't believe how much you two have grown since I left. Wendy, I do declare you have grown up so much. You have turned into a beautiful young woman."

Wendy held her reaction to the returned stepmother at bay. She would see how hurt dad was, before she graced her stepmother with her acceptance again.

When a private moment arose, Amy whispered to her mom, "Is it all over?"

Grace smiled at her, "It is. Thank you for your prayers. I couldn't have done it without you."

Travis built a fire that night, and they all gathered around it after supper. Before long, it was as if mom had never been gone. The newborn was doing his usual sleeping with one interruption right at bedtime.

Three weeks from Grace's arrival home, another letter came from the state penitentiary. Travis was not home to intercept it, so Grace received it. However, she did not open it. It didn't interest her what this man had to say. She tossed the unopened envelope into the fire. She wanted no reminders for her husband of this tragic episode. God had given her this perfect bliss, and she would not have it ruined for anything.

Isaiah went to the family doctor for his four-week checkup. He had gained almost five pounds. He proved to be a very healthy boy. His eyes had turned brown, like his dad's, and his feet were identical as well. He truly was his father's child. The doctor gave a good report.

However, he was not as pleased with Grace. "I remember specifically telling you not to have children, Grace." He chided, "Since your bout of cancer was as it is, I told you it would not be good for your health to get pregnant. You need to schedule an appointment with the nurse, so that I may check you out thoroughly," but Grace ignored his commands.

Haven Of Grace

Grace received a beckoning from Albert Jameston. He insisted on her coming to the old farm. They were in the process of building the new building, but they needed her approval on something important. She did not want to make this trip with her husband. He knew nothing of where she had been during those missing months, and she did not care for him to find out. She explained to him that she was going to a new building site for another foundation for work, which was not a lie.

Travis was highly reluctant about letting her get away from him so soon. He loved her being at home with Isaiah, when he came home from work. He had hoped she had put this job behind her for good, but he could not refuse her anything, so he allowed her this trip without much ado.

Albert was waiting at the airport for his favorite employee. A smile was spread from ear to ear, when he laid eyes on the bouncing baby boy. He drew both into his arms.

The chatting was idle on the way to the old farm. He asked many questions about the birth, and how things had been going for the new family. This occupied most of the miles. She was curious about his need for her to be here, but deemed it best to wait until he mentioned it.

The drive down the old familiar drive was different than any Grace had ever taken. The house and all remnants of it were gone. It was amazing how much freedom she felt from simply having that gone. Sure the old barn held some horrors, but something about the house had held her soul in obsequious fear. Wow! What independence came with the absence of the house! Neither brother or father could intimidate her now.

As they drove the last few yards of the driveway, Grace's eyes fell upon a large sign painted in elegant lettering, *Grace for Children Haven of Rest.* Beneath was added, *Owned by the Hope for Grace Foundation.* Albert watched the girl closely. He watched her swipe a quick tear from her cheek. When she had lived in this nightmare, not so long ago, she never would have dreamed this would be happening today. The years of torment, and the eight months of agony seemed to melt away. It was a glorious welcome.

Mr. Jameston bore a solemn look as he cut the engine. Grace had not noticed, heretofore, the squad car pulling in behind them. When she did notice, she looked to Mr. Jameston for an answer. He smiled, while helping her and Isaiah out of the car.

Buried Grace

"There is something very important we need you to look at. If it weren't important, I would not have called you back so soon. You see, we began construction last Wednesday, which was all fine and well, until they started digging the footings for the foundation." He held her arm gently, as she passed over some objects on the ground. "Watch your step. Grace, this is Officer Baker. We called him as soon as the men called me. He needed to ask you some questions."

"My, you have my curiosity up," Grace expressed. "I am anxious to see what this is."

The officer interpolated, "You may not be, after you it. Do you have a weak stomach, Mrs. Winston?" He waited for her response, and then proceeded to pull the plastic from a hole they had dug.

Grace did not give them the response they expected. Instead, her brows knit together in deep thought. "I don't understand. Who is it?"

"That is what we were hoping you could tell us," said the policeman. "Have you any ideas?"

"May I get a closer look?"

"By all means," he responded.

"Mr. Jameston, will you hold Isaiah?" he gently obliged. Grace crept closer, kneeling on the ground. She inspected the site carefully, before standing up. "I am not sure. Have you been able to determine an approximate time of death?"

"By the style of her clothing, thirty years, maybe longer. The colors have faded into the damp soil, but they are still observable."

"Can you tell what the cause of death was?"

The lawman reached in his vest pocket and pulled out a plastic bag. He held it out to her. Inside was a bullet. "We found this, embedded in the skull. We are still investigating. What do you think happened?"

Then, Grace thought deep and hard. It was an awfully long time ago. Her first question was to Mr. Jameston, but then her words seemed to be more for her own hearing, than any one else's.

"What part of the house was built over this spot?"

Mr. Jameston offered, "I believe part of the porch."

"No, it couldn't be. Could it? He said he built it as a memorial for her, because she had always wanted a wrap around porch. He only regretted not having built it before she died." She shook her head, "No, it couldn't be." Again, she knelt to her knees to scrutinize the bones again. On the fourth finger of her left hand, a gold band hung loosely around the bone.

"What is it? Do you know something?" the officer asked.

"I am not sure what is real."

"Well, anything would be helpful at this point. If we could at least identify the body, then we could maybe determine the cause of death."

Albert Jameston came close to Grace, who had climbed out of the hole. He wanted to support her in these hard decisions. "Who do you think it could be, Grace?"

She sighed, "There is a possibility, small as it may be, that it could be my mother."

The officer looked in surprise. "Tell me why you would think that?"

Grace looked sad. "When I was very young, she disappeared. My dad said she went to the hospital. About a week later, he told us she had died. I was young, like I said, but I don't recall a funeral. I have no idea where she could possibly be buried. It is worth a shot, I suppose. It is a jump off point."

"Where would dental records be? Do you remember who your dentist was at that point? What about doctor? Do you know the name of the hospital she was sent to?"

"I am sorry. I was very young. I may be mistaken, but I believe we changed all of that after her death. I boxed up a lot of papers from the house. They are mostly in storage. Some, I am afraid, I destroyed, but we could filter through the ones I kept. Who knows? Maybe we could come up with something valuable from them."

"Mrs. Winston, can you think of anyone else it could be, if it isn't your mother?"

Grace thought hard before answering. "I rightly don't know of anyone else. The more we speak of it, the more I get this sinking feeling in the pit of my stomach that it is she. It would make sense."

"Do you know anyone who would have wanted her gone? Why would anyone hurt her?"

"I am sure I don't know."

Grace Bound Changes

Grace felt more burdened down leaving, than when she came. The mystery before her seemed far fetched. It was like a dream, as if it was a story on the news. She feared that the truth was that her dad killed her mother.

That did not seem to fit. One thing she knew about him was that he loved her mother very much. She didn't understand why his perversion for children could not keep him committed to a healthy adult marriage, but she remembered how he looked at her mom.

Jameston drove her to make arrangements to have all the stored items sent to Oregon. Now, there was no point in paying for storage, when she could keep them at the farm. As soon as they arrived, she would begin searching through each item carefully.

Albert was heading back to New York, while Grace headed home. Until the authorities found some viable results, they could be of no use here.

Travis was more than relieved to receive the call of her plane returning. He sent her on one of Sinclair's personal private planes, while knowing it would bring her home sooner.

Prior to ten months ago, he never minded Grace's trips. She had gone many times to other cities or states for her job, but now, all that had changed. The thought of losing her forever had broken him of wanting his wife to ever go anywhere again without him. A joy filled him at the news that his wife and son were returning.

During her short trip, Renee and James returned from their elongated honeymoon. During her hiatus, James fell for Renee so hard that he jumped ship from the DA's office and was now working for Jameston.

Renee was more than pleased to see her sister-in-law had come home for good. The changes happening around the farm were of the delightful nature. To the thrill of everyone, Michelle's adoption was finalized during her absence. Travis had fought long and hard during Grace's absence to keep custody of Michelle. The social services were reluctant after Grace left, but Travis insisted that he could and would raise them perfectly fine, with or without Grace.

The days grew longer for the new mother. She was unable to perform the normal duties. It became harder and harder to make it through the day without lying down to take a nap. Her physical strength was fading. It became a routine to wait for everyone to leave for the day and Grace would take advantage of Isaiah's sleeping habits and go back to bed.

When she did get up for the day, she limited her physical work. She just did not have the strength as she once did. When the boxes from North Carolina came, she spent her days accomplishing that task.

Grace To Decipher

Finally! Every paper had been scrutinized to the tiniest detail. The only information she gleaned was a faded copy of some sort of bill from a Strickland, Whitmire, and Bowling office. Whether these were lawyers or not, it didn't say. She couldn't even find the name of their old doctor.

However, when she called the officer, he had already acquired that information, and the comparisons had been made. They had gone to the family's doctor of late and found to whom they had sent for Grace and Shawn's medical history. The doctor's office looked and found it easily.

The tests proved that it was the remains of Tammy Sorenson they found. The jury was still out as to whether or not it was homicide. They had sent the skeleton to the forensics lab for testing.

Grace needed a solution to this puzzle. Her mother had been buried beneath their house. The million-dollar question was why? What was the old man going to tell her, before he up and died on her? Daddy sure had a lot of dirty little secrets.

She had the idea to contact the private investigator that had found Angel and Ted's mother for her. He promised to get to the bottom of it for her. She gave him the name of the firm on the bill, along with the foreign address printed on it.

Grace was not too hopeful that any of these people could help her. The address was in a county eighty miles away from the old hometown. All she could do now is sit and wait.

She had settled into a routine. She spent as much time during the day with Isaiah, and then worked with Amy and Michelle, after school, teaching them how to perfect their riding skills.

She desired to give them an outlet for when the reality of life really hit them. As children reach a certain age, they begin to feel the repercussions of the traumas of life. Some day, Michelle will have to deal with killing her father. Travis had obviously made the transition easy for her, and life was simple, for now.

Amy, too, would someday understand the abominations that happened to her. Both girls would have a choice to make at that time. Some children choose drugs or alcohol to numb their pain, while others choose something healthy to occupy their time, in order to gain power over it. She intended to give them both a healthy choice.

Travis's happiness was renewed. He had never dreamed how wonderful life could be for him. This is the life he visualized he would have with the woman he loved. He showered her with tender love and care. However hard he tried to ease her load, he could not prevent the dark circles from forming under her eyes. She was able to hide her waning strength from him, but not Ruth. Ruth saw it all.

Exposition Lacking Grace

She confronted Grace one day in the nursery about always keeping Travis in the dark about the important things.

"You can't expect him to doo the right thing, if he doon't not know anything."

"It is not my intent to keep anything from him, Ruth. Some things are better unspoken, but in general, I don't wish to keep him in the dark. I just do not believe that the appropriate time has come for me to tell him. There are things that are difficult to say, especially without a purpose of saying them."

"Then, ya need to make an appropriate time."

"It is not that easy. There are things too unbelievable for me, let alone for someone else. There are things that I don't remember one day, and then the next, they come flooding into my memories, knocking my senses loose. There are days in which, I really battle with sanity, Ruth. It scares me."

Ruth put her arm around her. "You'll be fine, Lamby."

"I know. It is just that, when I think I have cleared the hurdle, the next one doubles in size. You spend your whole life loving and respecting someone, needing them, and then, you wake up one day and remember that person was not who you spent your whole life admiring."

"I know you aren't talking about Laddie."

Grace stood to put Isaiah in the crib. He had fallen asleep nursing. Grace leaned over the side of the crib and patted his tiny back. Sorrow crept in her half sobbing voice. "I don't remember how old I was. I do know that it was when I was very young." She shook her head. "I know it is just the devil. I have forgiven and shouldn't remember."

"What is it? What makes it coom back?"

"The reason for my last trip was to identify the remains of a human skeleton found buried under the old farm house I lived in when I was a child. I received confirmation last week that the skeleton was the remains of my mother. I never could remember her funeral. Now, I find out the reason for that is because there was none. She was buried beneath the porch like some animal caught in a trap." She finished patting Isaiah back to sleep and walked to the window. Her sad gaze looked out unseeingly. "I suppose that is what triggered it." She whispered," She knew. She... knew what he was doing to me. How could a mother see that and never say a word?"

287

"Ooh Lamby."

"I remember seeing her face and thinking, 'Now he'll have to stop. She'll not let him hurt me anymore. Thank God she walked in when she did.' She didn't stop him, though. Instead, she left me without an advocate."

A kind loving hand caressed her shoulder in sympathetic understanding. Then arms embraced her in comfort. Travis held her until her body stopped trembling beneath him. Ruth slipped out as not to be an intruder of this private moment.

He forced her to look into his eyes. "It's over. No one is going to hurt you anymore. You are the most precious thing in the world to me. Please don't think about the horrible past that is so painful to you. I cannot stand to see these beautiful eyes look like that."

The salt fell on her lips. "I am so sorry."

"No, no, no, no, no, no. You are not to be sorry. Look at me. Look at our son. You certainly have nothing to be sorry for. I love you, so much." Once again, he held her tight, only longer this time. They huddled over the crib, until the sounds of Amy and Michelle broke the spell. Travis kissed Grace's hair. "Oh, the reason I came in was to tell you some man by the name of Simms called you, wanting you to call back. I left the

288

number by the phone in the living room.

After Grace collected herself again, she ran downstairs to call the investigator back. She was anxious to find out what he had uncovered.

"Mrs. Winston. I have been able to track down the office of Strickland, Whitmire, and Bowling. This was a firm of psychiatrists. The eldest is dead, but she saw Strickland. He has retired. It seems she spent some time in the psychiatric ward prior to her disappearance. There is little other information in which I could obtain without you. The office is expecting you to arrive in the next couple of days. They will release the information to only you. They are bound by law to keep confidentiality. I am afraid that it doesn't sound very good Mrs. Winston. I think you should get there quickly."

Single Act of Grace

After long debate, Grace invited her husband to join her on
the expedition. It was by mutual consent, after a long
discussion. It was hard for Grace to open up enough to divulge
part of her secrets to anyone. She was used to sharing all with
her heavenly Father, but another person was another story. She
did not share everything. She still didn't tell him where she had
spent those eight months.

Ruth was right. One thing she learned from all of this was
that she needed to open up to her husband, some. They could
never be one her, if she kept schisms between them, as Ruth had
expressed very clearly.

They decided to leave the next morning. Grace was having
anxiety from leaving Isaiah so soon. He was so young and had
never been away from her more than an hour at a time, but Ruth
reassured her she would take care of all her children as if they
were her own. They laughed at the new mother's nervousness.

Amy felt more secure about her mom's leaving this time.
She knew if dad was going, then it would be a short trip. The
ever-romantic Renee insisted it was their wedding trip, but
Travis and Grace knew the real reason for the trip.

They all gathered on the back porch for a spring barbeque as a bon voyage. James was churning the ice cream maker, while Renee looked longingly into his eyes. Amy and Michelle were atop Samson and Ginger. Ruth and Grace were in the kitchen, while Travis was gathering some firewood for the cool of the even.

He was the first to hear a car in the drive, and then Grace wiped her hand and went to the door. She watched her husband dealing with a strange man just beneath the steps.

She was falling in love with him all over again. He knew all her defects and still loved her unconditionally. There he stood in all his strength and glory. The sun softening his brown locks, his jaws demonstrating his determination showed her that no other would ever be her perfect soul mate.

The look, however, on his face upon his return was not one of jovial nature. He shut the door with a slump in his shoulders. He grabbed his wife and held her tight, as if he never intended to let go. The sweet beckoning of Isaiah wanting to be fed or changed interrupted the moment.

Grace excused herself and ran to her son. She felt a twinge of regret, because Travis really looked as if something was bothering him. She need not feel bad long, though, because momentarily he followed her into the nursery.

"Grace, I don't know how to tell you this. I have tried to keep all this away from you, but it appears that I can't do that any longer."

Out of character, she pulled her husband's strong cheek to her lips. "I love you. I don't know if it is possible to love someone more every single day, yet I do. I think you grow more handsome every time I look at you. Our time on earth is as a vapor, but I know I could never have been blessed with a better husband."

Travis became flushed, forgetting for the moment his quest. He gathered her close, treasuring the joy in her violet eyes. "What did I do to deserve you? You are so precious to me."

"Now, what is it you tried to keep from me, but can no longer?"

His warm smile faded, while he handed her a paper, "Singleton has been harassing you, since you have been away. I know it was wrong of me to open them, but I couldn't help it. He is a scoundrel who wants to torment you further. Now, he has the audacity to try and sue you for visitation of our son."

"Don't worry, my dear husband. God be for us, who can be

against us?"

Grace read the note attached to the subpoena. Singleton was demanding visitation to his child, since he was imprisoned for rape, he might as well claim the kid. Grace sent Travis out to enjoy the barbeque with the rest of the family, while she gathered her infant son and slipped away from the party to stop Singleton once and for all.

Travis may have rejoined the gala, but he was not joyous. He was constantly praying for God to take this discomfort from his family. He shrugged a smile whenever someone asked him what had happened to mom or Grace. He wasn't even sure.

She didn't disappear for long, though. Within an hour she had returned as if nothing had happened at all. The baby lay snug in his crib, sleeping as if nothing had changed within the hour. Grace came from the kitchen with the fresh apple pie, which she pulled out of the oven.

"Oh, Mom, the ice cream is just ready. It will be delicious with this pie," cried Michelle.

Grace hugged Ruth. "You know, the best pie maker in the world made this especially for you and your dad. She knew it was your favorite."

293

"How long are you two going to be gone on this trip?" James asked, as he popped a fresh strawberry in his mouth.

Travis answered, "We don't know. It should be just a few days. Why?"

He looked mischievously at his own wife, took her hand in his, and grinned. "Your sister and I thought that if you two were going to be gone through the weekend, we might take our favorite nieces down to Disney Land for the weekend. Maybe let them skip school Friday, and we could leave Thursday evening. What do you say? We would offer to take the little guy, but being that he wouldn't enjoy it, and Ruth would be lost without him, we figured it would be better not to offer."

The girls, Wendy included, jumped up joyously. In unison, Amy and Michelle shouted, "Please?"

Dad looked at mom. He was not about to make that decision without mom. Mom smiled and gave them a hug. "We'll see. I will let you know before we leave."

That night, after the children had gone to bed, and Grace was giving Isaiah his last feeding for the night, she consented to allow the children to go to Disney Land. She really wished she could have been the one to take them. There may not be time later on for showing them how much fun she was. She didn't

294

want to cheat them out of having fun. Life was too short not to be spontaneous once in a while.

Travis's Journey With Grace

She and Travis left very early the next morning. She nursed Isaiah one last time, before grudgingly leaving him. The Sinclair plane was fueled and ready to take them on their journey, and was well on the way before the sun rose in its nest.

Grace began feeling nervous. She was not sure what she was going to find, but the old demons could no longer hurt her. Her knight was with her this time. She wanted to hunt the truth about what happened to her mother. Did the old man kill her? Was that what he was trying to tell her the night he died? If so, should she absolve him from that as well? "Lord, help me, please. I need Thy guidance," she prayed without ceasing.

She didn't want to waste a minute once they arrived. Travis wanted to stop for dinner, but Grace pleaded to go on. Travis won the argument by getting her to agree to a lunch date, but to his chagrin, Grace only picked at her meal. She was too anxious to eat much. Her stomach kept flip-flopping uncontrollably. She wanted to find the truth.

Her palms were sweaty as she walked into the office building of Strickland, Whitmire, and Bowling. Travis slid her hand through his arm and held his other hand on hers and prepared to be a rock for her no matter the outcome.

She spoke quietly, "I would like to speak to Dr. Whitmire. I do not have an appointment."

The receptionist politely answered, "What is your name?"

"Grace Sorenson Winston."

"Oh yes. He was expecting you. He left these for you. I just need to see some identification. This is highly unusual. Dr. Whitmire wanted me to express to you, that if you had not had these court orders, he would not be allowed to release any information to anyone. He did not like being summoned."

"I understand, and thank you," Grace smiled her charm. She penned her name and received the folder. "Please express to Dr. Whitmire my deepest appreciation. What is found here will be considered confidential to only the police."

"It is no skin off my nose, but I'll tell him." With that, the woman shut the small window between them.

Grace looked at her husband, "Shall we?"

He led her to their hotel room, where Grace settled down with the folder. She looked at him for support, where he kissed her head. Side by side, they looked at the doctor's notes:

03/12 - Initial consultation - New patient suffering from depression and neurosis. Mrs. Sorenson has found irrevocable problems in her marriage and wants to divorce husband. Patient expresses fear of husband. Signs of paranoia demonstrate patient believes husband holds some power over her that compels her to bid his wishes. Erratic outbursts exhibits patient fears for the safety of her children, but she has given me no reason for suspecting the husband of violent tendencies. Next visit, we will try to work on the issues at the base of her neurosis.

03/24...

04/05...

04/30 - Patient dropped by the office in hysterics. Subjected patient to hypnosis to determine origin of hysteria. Per results of hypnosis, I have admitted patient into the Meadow Downs facility for short-term observation, after patient showed suicidal tendencies. I believe she is a danger to herself.

05/02 - Patient has been willing thus far with committing to the therapy. She has asked, however, to be able to leave for the time it would take to get her children to safety. I am not sure if the fear of the husband is a psychosis or paranoia. I have suggested she continue her in-house treatment for the time being.

05/05 - After an attack of hysterics, Patient walked out of session today A.M.A. Patient stated she would return in a few days to complete treatment. I am not convinced patient is mentally stable or that she is not a threat to herself or others.

That was it. It ended there. There were no more pages. What now? What did all this mean? Could her mother have been capable of suicide? The question was if she had committed suicide, then why was her body buried under the house? She could not have buried herself. Suicide would have been a legitimate way to die. He would not have had to hide a suicide. Why would she leave Grace alone, if she knew? How could she leave Grace alone, if she knew? No, he had to have killed her, but why?

Travis handed her back the last page, silently. It was definitely an awkward moment. Neither completely understood at what they were looking.

"Mr. Simms said that Strickland was her doctor, and he is retired. Maybe if we could find him and talk with him, he could shed some light. I need to know, did my father kill my mother, or did she commit suicide?"

Travis pulled the phone book from the drawer. Flipping through the pages, he found what he was looking for. "There are two William Strickland's in here. They both live on the same road. Maybe one is the father and the other is the son. We can check them both out. Shall we go?"

Grace placed her hand on his arm. "Thank you for being here. You don't know what it means to me that you are here for this."

"Don't thank me. I have done nothing short of loving you." He touched her cheek. "You make doing that so very simple."

While they were waiting for the elevator to open, Travis looked upon his wife. She had dark circles under her eyes, and her shoulders sagged slightly. He put his hand on her shoulder and guided her back down the hallway. "This can wait," he reported confidently.

"I really want to do this today," Grace pleaded.

He shook his head. "You are tired. We are still on Oregon time. You can hardly stand. Tomorrow will give you another opportunity to get all the information you need. Come on. We'll call our children and settle down for the evening. We can get up early in the morning to get started."

Grace didn't like it, but did not refuse. She allowed him to lead her back into the hotel room. She *was* tired. She had not stopped long enough to realize just how tired she was. The long flight and day had caught up with her. It was still rather early, but she could enjoy an early evening with her husband.

Poetry Of Grace

They each took a hot shower. Travis would order some supper later, but Grace was ready to call it a night.

She perched on the window seat brushing her hair, while concentrating on a woodpecker's red head bopping back and forth to the tune of rat a tat. It brought back another place in time, when she would sit on her bed, as a little girl, and stare out the window, wishing she were a bird flying free or that squirrel that could get in and out of any small place. Many times she had wished to be someone else or something else, anybody except who she really was.

Travis emerged from the bathroom and saw the pretty picture. She was stroking her hair unknowingly. Her hair was soft beneath his palm, her skin like velvet, when his fingers touched her cheek. He was aware of the sadness that had developed a home in the lovely violet eyes. There was once a carefree confidence defying any limitations, but somewhere, at some point, the fleeting assurance diminished.

"Sweetheart."

"Yes," was the distant response.

He fell on his knees, looking up to her beautiful violet eyes. "I know what you mean. You were talking the other day about each day bringing a stronger more defined love. That is exactly how I feel about you. Just when I think you are so incredible and amazing, I find something new and more awesome about you."

There was a remnant of the once glorious charm in her smile, which had faded in the aftermath of such a battle as she had been facing. "You exaggerate my glory, because you are most definitely prejudice." She became lost in the admiration of his soft brown eyes. "Our son is so very fortunate."

"How so?"

"One day, he will grow up to be the spitting image of his dad. He looks so much like you now. He has your eyes. Just imagine, one day, there will be some young girl gazing into his eyes and declaring her undying love for him. I wish...I hope, when he comes home with his wife, she will feel about him the way his mother feels about his dad. I pray that he will be truly happy."

"No woman will ever hold a candle to you. I believe you and I have the most unique love ever imaginable. He could only hope for a woman like you."

Grace returned to gazing dreamily out into the gorgeous day. "Your dad not being there while you were growing up didn't seem to effect you negatively. If anything, I believe it made you stronger, emotionally. I hope Isaiah can be like that."

"I hope he never has to find out. I don't plan on going anywhere any time soon."

"I pray not."

Travis opened the book of love in his heart. The unparalleled passion within could not be contained. "You are my beloved. You know, we never appreciate what we have, until it is gone. I found out the hard way how very much I adore you. I never want to experience life without you again. We have kept so many things from each other over the years, and in turn have cheated our love."

"I agree. God gave me a helpmeet. You can't help, if you're kept in the dark." She cupped his strong face in her dainty hands. "I love you and my precious babies more than my own life. You may not believe it, and I know I can never take her mother's place, but Wendy is precious to me as well."

"I believe it. That is what I am talking about. You won Wendy's heart. Granted, she wasn't happy, when we thought you had left for good, but even then, she continued to grow in her love. They missed you so much. Amy and Michelle would pray together every night before bed. I overheard them a couple times. They both prayed fervently for their mom to be able to come home soon and to watch over you with extra care."

"What about you? Did you pray for mom as well?"

"Harder than I have ever prayed for anyone in my life." He kissed her gently, "No more secrets?"

"No more secrets," she murmured. Breathless from his intoxicating touch, she closed her eyes to make a memory of it.

He pushed her far enough away to be able to focus on her face. "I think it is odd that you know everything about my life. You even know things about my life and family I didn't know. You made a point to know all about me, but I never knew much about you, like why you were living with your uncle or why you left home. When we were kids, I was too busy with my own problems to find out. All I know of your past is what I have assumed and guessed. I think it is time to put the guesswork behind."

The two talked till after midnight. Grace kept only where she had been during her pregnancy from her husband. She did not deem this a secret, for it was for the best interest of her girls that no one ever knew.

By this time, the two had retired and almost asleep, when Grace revealed one last secret.

"Travis," she deliberately whispered. "I have one more secret."

"Hmmm," he grunted half asleep.

"I am not going to take the treatments this time."

Unanswered Grace

Doctor Strickland remembered Tammy Sorenson very well.
As a matter of fact, she had tormented his sleep for many years.
The hollowed darkened eyes the last night he saw her and the
hysterical cries that had forthwith exploded from her diaphragm,
as the injection was given to her, had given him many sleepless
hours over the years.

The old man shook terribly with age, but his mind seemed
clear as water. "You have her eyes." He spoke in a rough old
faded voice, "You don't look much like her, except in the eyes.
Don't look at me!" he snapped, as a memory hurled viciously.

"Can you tell me about the last time you saw my mother? It
is important, that we find out about her condition that night."

He shook and bent his head. Grace thought he was either
not going to tell, or he did not hear her at all. He began slowly,
"It was two weeks before I had my stroke. She came to me in
tears crying incoherently. We gave her an injection to
tranquilize her. We were not sure whether what she told us that
night was true or not. All we could do was listen. She told a
tale that could only be make believe."

Grace touched his arm lightly. He crooked his head, searching carefully for his sanity. Standing before him was the answer to the years of questions. He continued. "Was it true? What she said that night, was it true?"

"Please," she urged softly. "She died within the week. We need to know why she died."

"She feared for her life. She said she did not know her husband anymore. She wanted to take her little boy and you and leave, but she was afraid he would stop her. I suppose he did." He shook his head. "It is all my fault."

"How is it your fault? You couldn't have prevented her death."

The old man almost began to cry. "I diagnosed her as a paranoid neurosis. I ignored her pleas, thinking she was…in answer to your question, you are the reason she died."

"I beg your pardon?"

"She saw something she wasn't suppose to see. She tried to get help, but apparently it was too late. You must understand, in those days, people just didn't do those kinds of things, or no one knew what to do about it. I thought she was just hysterical. I am sorry for your mother's death, but surely you cannot hold me responsible."

"No sir. I don't hold you responsible for anything. Please, anything you can tell us will be helpful. Is it possible that her husband could have killed her?"

"That is what she was afraid of. Whether he could or not, I don't know. I never met the man. I tended to lean more to suicide. She was weak spirited. On the few occasions in which I spoke with her, she spoke of giving up. Had it not been for her girl and boy, she would have given up a long time before she did."

"Doctor, what would her means have been?"

"She dreamed about being in a car and flying carefree, as if the car wore wings, until a bright light beckoned her to come. She claimed that would be the only peace she could ever find."

"Thank you for your time, sir." Grace accepted Travis's arm as the two departed.

"You have found your answers, haven't you?" he asked, while preparing for a shower.

"I am afraid I'll never know, until I reach Home."

Travis frowned. "But, you suspect?"

309

"All I have are suspicions. I wouldn't doubt my dad's ability to murder her. It fits like a glove, but I have this inexplicable feeling that she did this to herself. The only reason I could imagine him burying her beneath the house would be to hide his crime. Why else would he lie about her dying? None of it makes a bit of sense. I spoke with the local sheriff while you were in the shower."

"What did he say?"

"Forensics showed that she was shot at point blank range. He said it was possible that it was self-inflicted, but there is no conclusive answer. If he murdered her, it doesn't matter. The past is the past. It cannot be undone or changed. You cannot send a dead man to prison. We will just close this case unresolved."

"I know you hate coming all this way and not find the answer."

She smiled wearily, "It hasn't been for nothing. I have gotten to know my husband better. Are you ready to go? I miss my family."

They threw the couple of articles of clothing left out into the suitcase. Travis took this opportunity to steal a kiss in private. "Forgive me, my love, but you still looked worried." He held the door open for her.

"I'm not worried about her death." She still wore a sad expression. "It is after her death that breaks my heart. In speaking to the doctor, I am doubting I will ever see her in Heaven."

Grace For Completion

Several hours later, Travis was more than surprised, when the Sinclair plane landed, but it was not the Eugene skyline before him.

After his wife explained that they were taking a side trip, she hailed a cab to the state penitentiary. Inside, they went through the normal search routine for visitors, before being allowed to enter. It was not normal visiting times, but after Grace spoke privately with the man in charge, they were seated in a large room, which contained several long tables.

Here, they waited almost twenty minutes until Ron Singleton was finally before them. He had a smirk of annoying control. He assumed he had the dominating hand. He expected to see fear and angst in his opponent's eyes. Instead, he was met with true Irish fire.

"Mrs. Winston, it is nice to see you again," he sneered, looking at Travis, while trying to get them both riled up.

Travis looked at Grace. Did she expect him to take this man's smug attitude without saying anything? She relieved his tension, though. "Mr. Singleton, pleasantries do not become you. We all know exactly how pleased you are to see us, and frankly we do not care. We are here to inform you to stop writing letters and making absurd demands. I suggest you call your lawyer dog off, or you will be more embarrassed than you already are."

"Whatever do you mean? I have asked for nothing short of the right to claim my own son. By the way, I am so happy for a boy. I was afraid to hope for one, but you pulled it off."

Travis could no longer withhold his tongue, "You have no claim on our son. You leave him alone." Grace placed her hand on his knee and squeezed, giving him a loving and reassuring look.

"What my husband is saying is, Isaiah is our son not yours. If you insist upon pushing this issue, you will be reviewed as a man still trying to rape little children. Unless you want your prison term longer than it already is, then I suggest you leave my family alone."

He chuckled an evil laugh, "Oh, but the fun is just beginning. It doesn't matter if Winston adopts my kid. It doesn't change the fact that he is mine, and I have every right to him."

Grace smiled at her husband and stood to leave. "I really feel sorry for you Mr. Singleton. You have no remorse for destroying so many little lives. We stopped you once before, and we are stopping you again." She reached in her purse and pulled out some papers and laid them on the table. "You must think I am a fool, if you think I came here unprepared. You cannot have my son. These blood test results will be sent to your attorney as well. Hang them on your cell wall and look at them everyday. I want you to know and suffer from the results of my son's paternity test. Good day, Mr. Singleton."

Coming To Terms With Grace

Because of the late hour, they decided to spend the night in Portland. When Travis came out of the shower and Grace was perched on the sofa, with knees hugged to her chest, it reminded him of the night of the class reunion. Could it be possible that she was even more beautiful now? He supposed all men thought such thoughts, after their beloved had given him a child. He was so proud of her today. She showed nothing but determination to that slime bag. It was a hint of her former self.

He paused in front of the window. The city lights below twinkled merrily. What a concept? Grace, in her former glory. He told her he would rather spend a limited time with her love, than a lifetime without it, and God was certainly putting that to the test. He would live each day as if it were the last. The quality of life was most valuable.

He ventured, "How long have you known, Grace?"

"About the cancer?"

"Yes."

"The symptoms started a little after Isaiah was born."

"What does the doctor say about it?"

"The doctor doesn't know what he is talking about."

"Why?"

"Travis, had I listened to him, we would not have our son. I would gladly give my life over ten times for our son."

"You haven't been back to the doctor?" Grace shook her head. "Then how can you be sure?"

"I just know. They never really got it all in the first place."

"Then, I am putting my foot down this time. First thing, when we get back, we will get you an appointment and get this thing under control."

The wife slipped gracefully to his side and put her hand on his shoulder. "Not this time, dear."

"I insist," he spoke with a weakening defense, but he could not fight her stubbornness. For reasons of her own, she had chosen not to fight. This angered him, but he could not be angry.

"What purpose would it serve? To prolong the suffering, or to extend the grief of my family? No. It's as it should be. I am prepared to journey this shadowed valley. My Comfort shall guide my way. I will not fear, and neither should you."

"What about Amy, Michelle, and Isaiah? Do you intend they should grow up without a mother?"

"It is not my intentions, beloved, but it is the path I must tread. God has the answers to all. It is not ours to ask questions. It is our job to run the race in faith, knowing He will have the victory over all. I will always thank Him for the sweet hours He gave me with you and the children. For us, we must prepare, together. The battle is not mine, because I am His. Victory will be the perfect healing."

That night the two held especially close to each other, fusing their souls as one for the valley ahead. Together, they chose not to tell anyone else at all about the cancer.

Secretly, Travis prayed for God to intervene and heal his lifeline. He did not want to live without her again. However, he knew beforehand what the answer was to be.

The Pall Of Grace

Late October came and cold weather was set in. Another year of harvest was completed. Of course, nothing would ever be as good as when Isaiah tilled the ground, but God blessed the increase.

Little Isaiah was bigger and beginning to get into more. He was just learning to stand on his own and beginning to walk. He was the most precious thing in Ruth's eyes. She loved Amy and Michelle, but her dear Isaiah's namesake was special.

This particular morning, Grace set out before daybreak to her prayer garden. She had begun to spend many hours there, since the pain had become excruciating. There were no medicines to vanquish the agony; therefore, she suffered in silence. Today she prayed to the Father aloud, crying for Him to ease her pain.

"Lord," she cried, "I don't want to fail you. I do not want to waiver in my faith. Please, help this wretched old sinner, saved by grace."

She saw the girls off to school, Travis and Wendy off to work, and then Ruth and Isaiah off to the grocery store. Weary, Grace took a midmorning nap. It was then, that the Lord answered her prayer. As she slept, she was transformed from her earthly body to her new perfect Heavenly body. As the last breath of this life left her, so did the pain of the accursed cancer. She was free! She would never suffer from illness again. She had run her race, and victory was won.

Her death was like her life. She wanted to spare those around her, and she did. It was her beloved Travis that found her. When she drew her last breath, an emptiness overwhelmed him, taking away his breath. He felt as if he were free falling in a bottomless dark pit. He felt her cross over as a feeling of isolation overtook him. He ran home and found a smile on her lips that he had not seen in years. Her smile of charm and peace showing a joy unspeakable and full of glory.

The Witness of Grace

"Isaiah, I wish you would reconsider going out tonight. There will be a lot of drunken kids roaming the streets. Your sisters and I wanted to take you out to celebrate."

The insolent reply came, "I am going with my friends. You worry too much, dad. It's my graduation, don't I deserve a party?"

"But son..."

"I know your buts dad. You probably want me to go to some old church on my night. I didn't slave over school for thirteen years to go to church. That was yours and mom's thing, don't drag me into it."

"I can't force you to do anything. I am just glad your mother is not here to see this." He went to his room and returned momentarily. He held out an object to his son. "This is suppose to be given to you on your eighteenth birthday, but I think it would be okay to give it to you now."

Travis sighed sadly and walked out the door, casting one last pleading look over his shoulder. He went to the prayer garden and paced over the graves. Over the years, he had taken up his wife's habit of wearing a path in the prayer garden. God was the only One that could change his son's heart.

The young man slammed his bedroom door behind him and automatically turned up the stereo. His dad hated it when he listened to this music; therefore, he would sound it loud just to irritate him. He threw the yellow package on the bed and took his shower. His dad was always out there ranting over his mother's grave. Praying as if that would bring her back. He hated his mother for having left him, and he blamed his dad. He was not going to serve this hateful God that took his mother.

It was not until he was almost dressed that he spotted and remembered the package. At first, he was not going to open it, because his dad gave it to him, but the penmanship on the front grabbed his attention and would not release the grip on his heart.

Inside was a cassette tape with his name written on it. He had remembered that Amy had received a similar package on her eighteenth birthday. The thought that it came from his mother, made his heart leap in contrast to the hatred he wanted to feel.

Against the desires of his own will, he put the tape in and pressed play. For the first time in his memory, he heard his mother's voice.

"My dear sweet Isaiah, you have reached your eighteenth birthday. How very proud I am of you! I am looking at you in my mind, and I see you so very handsome. You look just like dad. You have his soft trusting eyes. That is what made me fall in love with him and with you. Whenever he looked at me with those beautiful brown eyes, I could refuse him nothing. If you could have seen him the day he found out he had a son, you would truly know how much he loves you. That is why you should be so proud to look like him and to be like him. I can think of no greater role model.

I pray you follow in his footsteps. He is a wonderful father, and I know you are a good son. *The fear of the Lord is the beginning of knowledge: A wise son heareth his father's instruction: but a scorner heareth not rebuke.* Listen to your dad. He will never tell you anything to hurt you. He loves you so much. If you don't believe me, just ask your sisters. One thing I know. He sacrificed the things dearest to him for you.

As you venture out into adulthood, I want you to remember your raising. I know your dad brought you up in church and you know the Truth. I trust in my Heavenly Father to lead you in the right direction. You are about to face the biggest choices you will ever have to make. You are at the crossroads of your life. Pray hard for wisdom, and He will never fail you.

The world has a pull that is demanding and attractive. It can offer you many things. It can give you the pleasures of sin, for a season. It is so tempting to be offered lots of money, beautiful women, and everything your heart desires. You must remember though, Satan tempted Christ in the same ways. It is how we choose that makes all the difference in the world.

When you meet that one special girl, Isaiah, make sure she is as pure as you are. It is important for you to marry your equal. Marriage takes hard work from both man and wife. Anything worth having is worth working for. I hope she feels about you the same way I feel about your dad. I pray that she is honest and decent. She should desire to love your family as much as you should love hers.

Isaiah, do not be resentful and angry toward me for leaving. You cannot blame your dad or anybody else. Especially, do not blame God. I will have been here almost eighteen years by the time you are hearing this, and I assure you, I am living in a perfect body and running the streets of gold. I didn't leave you willingly. I would rather have been with you for many years, but my sinful body just could not handle it any longer. God delivered me from my suffering. Praise His name!

I was named Grace, because my mother said God graced her with a daughter, but Grace is a hard name to live up to. I have experienced real Heaven-sent grace from my Savior. Through the last few months, He has given me new grace, an amazing grace in which I have never known. In the song, Amazing Grace, listen to the last verse. *When we've been there ten thousand years, we have no less days to sing God's praise, than when we first begun.* Think about that for a minute and you will understand how amazing His grace can and will be. I would not have you, my son, miss out on His amazing grace.

I await my loved ones, here, where we shall spend eternity together. I had the glorious pleasure of seeing Amy and Michelle and Wendy saved. I know we will meet again. What about you, my sweet Isaiah? Will you be here with me, someday? Have you made that life altering choice? If not, now is the time to choose whom you will serve, man or God? What am I talking about? You are your father's son. Of course, you have already made that choice. I have no doubt I will see you here.

Good bye my beloved, in the words of a favorite hymn, *I will meet you in the morning, just inside the eastern gate over There.* Be wise in the Lord. Let Him guide your life, and I will meet you in the morning."

The graduation service exhibited proud parents of many young students, who were getting ready to venture into the cruel reality of living. None were prouder, though, than Amy, Michelle, Wendy, and Travis. Ruth would have been delighted over her godson, had she not been promoted on to Glory three years ago.

Isaiah stepped proudly up to accept his diploma. Travis could not help seeing Grace's mannerisms in his son. How sad he could not be more like her. Isaiah had his mother's charming smile and had unfortunately gotten away with a lot over the years by using it. As a parent, he had been way too lenient on the wayward son. He couldn't hear the words his son spoke as he held his diploma high. "This is for you, mom."

Hands resounding in applause concluded the graduation ceremony, and a mingled throng filled the room. Travis searched the crowd of gowns for one last attempt to plead with his son to come home. When at last he found him, Isaiah was talking to his friends.

To his dad's surprise, the son put his arm around him, "Thanks Tommy, but maybe some other night. Tonight, I'm going to spend time with my family. See you later."

The tears in the father's eyes were hidden behind the lids. "Thank You, God for answering another prayer."

Amy and her husband engulfed the two men first, followed by Wendy and her husband, and Michelle. From the core of the huddle, they heard him question, "Do we have a church meeting to go to or something? Mom is expecting me."

Made in the USA
Charleston, SC
08 July 2014